# by Stephen W. Meader

# STEPHEN W. MEADER

# THE SEA SNAKE

ILLUSTRATED BY EDWARD SHENTON

SOUTHERN SKIES

© 1943 HARCOURT BRACE & WORLD, INC.
© 1965 STEPHEN W. MEADER
© 2005 SOUTHERN SKIES LLC

All rights reserved

ISBN 978-1-931177-34-4 cloth
ISBN 978-1-931177-35-1 paperback

## *Dedication*

*The republication of this book is dedicated with love to Jennifer Atchley Cochran---extraordinary mother, thoughtful and loving daughter, trusted friend, graceful beauty, Daddy's girl---by her father who adores her, Jerry Atchley.*

# THE SEA SNAKE

# 1

THE loose, coarse sand was hot under Barney's bare feet. He could feel the burn of it even through the leathery calluses on his soles. It shifted under him as he climbed the dune, and the tough green wires of beach grass clutched at his ankles, but he moved steadily upward till he reached the crest.

From the height of the dune he could look northeast and southwest along one of the most desolate stretches on the whole Atlantic Coast. But it didn't seem lonely to Barney Cannon. He had lived all of his sixteen years on that thin sliver of land fringing the seaward side of the Carolina sounds.

In front of him was the broad beach and the blue-green sea. There was a light, steady wind, and the breakers came rolling in with a solemn roar. Offshore the gulls sailed and dipped and screamed. Three miles up the beach toward Kitty Hawk, lost now in the haze, there was a Coast Guard station. And the same distance in the opposite direction was the end of the land, where the inlet opened on the sound. Between them nothing was visible but empty beach and dune, sea and sky.

Barney went along the crest for fifty yards and came to a low canvas shelter covering a pit dug out of the side of the dune. The cloth was weathered to the color of the sand, and was practically invisible from a few steps away. From its rear a pair of wires trailed off unobtrusively to stakes among the beach grass.

"Hi, Evan," the boy announced his coming.

A head appeared from under the edge of the canvas. "Oh, that you, Barney? You're early, ain't you?"

"Five minutes, maybe. But you go ahead an' I'll take over. Any reports?"

"Three or four patrol planes. There's the sheet."

Evan Blake crawled out of the sand pit and stretched. He was a year or two older than Barney and one of the Cannons' few neighbors. "I better get on home," he said. "Paw'll want to go fishin'. You et yet?"

Barney shook his head. "Anna's going to bring me some

grub when it's ready. So long, now."

As the other lad departed he let himself down into the cool hollow in the sand. It was a snug enough place, once he was inside. A bench made of driftwood reached across it, and a heavy plank was set into the seaward side, forming a breast-high shelf. On the plank stood a telephone set, a rusty alarm clock, and a sheaf of ruled paper with a stub of pencil tied by a string. This was the equipment of Volunteer Lookout Post, "Lena Six," of the Army Fighter Command.

There were no glasses or binoculars, but Barney had good eyes. He had taken his turn at watching here every second day, month after month, ever since America had declared war.

The front opening of the shelter commanded a wide view of the ocean and the beach at either side and, by leaning out a little, Barney could see most of the sky. On a clear day he was sometimes able to spot ships and patrol planes as much as ten miles away.

He had been sitting there ten minutes or more when he heard the familiar throb of a radial engine overhead. He peered out, shading his eyes with his hand, and saw an observation plane, dark in its war paint, coming over at two thousand feet. He waved, and the pilot tilted his wings in greeting before he roared out to sea. It was Barney's friend, Lieutenant Slug Martin.

The boy picked up the telephone with one hand, and the pencil with the other. "Army Flash," he told the operator. In the ten seconds it took to put the call through, he was jotting symbols in the spaces on the ruled log sheet.

"Army. Go ahead, please," came the voice from headquarters. It was a woman's voice, cool and impersonal.

"One," answered Barney. "Single motor. Low. Seen. Lena Six. Northwest. Overhead. Southeast."

"Thank you," said the girl at the filter center, and Barney hung up with a mumbled "Welcome, ma'am."

He entered the time in the first space on the line—"12.08." The other columns were headed: Number of planes; number of motors; altitude; seen or heard; post code name; direction observed; distance from post; direction headed.

Slug Martin's plane was still visible, a tiny dark speck, four miles out over the Atlantic. Gradually it blended with the sky. He lost it once, found it again for a few seconds, and finally it was gone.

After another quarter hour of watching he caught the faint *swish, swish* of footsteps in the sand.

"Anna?" he called, and the girl answered with a laugh.

Her bright head with its straw-colored braids appeared at the edge of the canvas. "Always I try to surprise you, Barney," she said, "but your ears—they are too sharp."

She held out a covered tin pail. "It's fish chowder," she told him. "And still hot. *Ach*, ya—and a spoon to eat it with. I brought it in my pocket."

The girl sat beside him and chatted while he ate. She was two years younger than he, a brown, chubby youngster with a winning smile. Anna Kranz was Austrian. Back in the autumn she had been brought ashore, wet and bedraggled, from a torpedoed refugee ship. Barney's father had been out with the boat that day, and he helped bring in the few survivors. Mrs. Cannon's big heart went out to the orphaned girl the moment she saw her. She had lived with them ever since as one of the family, and gone to school with Barney all winter.

Anna was a bright child, quick and helpful, and she had picked up English at an amazing rate. Meanwhile she taught Barney enough German so that she could talk to him in her own tongue when she felt homesick. He had two older brothers, but a girl around the place was a novelty. It was like having a kid sister except that he was prouder of her accomplishments and quarreled with her less frequently.

"Gosh," he told her between mouthfuls, "this chowder sure is good. Bet you helped make it."

"I cut up the potatoes, very small, very nice," she grinned. "That is all I do to help because I cry too much when I try to cut onions! Let me taste it, Barney?"

"Why, sure," he answered, offering her the spoon. "Haven't you had dinner yet?"

She smacked her lips over the steaming broth and shook her blonde braids. "They keep it hot for me—don't you worry," she smiled. "But I must go pretty soon. Look, Barney, what's that ship out there?"

He had kept one eye on the sea while he ate. "The one you're pointing at looks like a destroyer," he told her. "Guarding a convoy, I reckon. You can see the others behind. Three—four—six freighters all bunched together, an' a couple o' smaller craft—subchasers, probably."

The girl's shoulders moved in an involuntary shiver. "Don't you have to tell about them on the telephone?" she asked.

"No—not unless one of 'em is sunk or in trouble," said Barney. "An' they generally make out all right, long as they stick together."

Anna rose, brushing the sand from her skirt. "I would be

sorry to see it happen," she sighed. "I grow sad when I think about it. I am going back now, Barney. And if you have finished, I'll take the pail and spoon."

When she was gone he sat for a long time, watching the distant convoy. Most of the ships were hull down over the horizon, but he could pick out the movements of the destroyer as her smoke cloud circled about the slower merchantmen. It was nearly half an hour before the fleet of ships passed out of sight to the northeastward.

Barney had learned to be patient, sitting there in the lookout station. He studied the drift of the clouds and the color of the sea, figuring out the weather. It ought to hold fair for another day, he thought. Always his ears were tuned for the hum of approaching airplane motors. The breeze fluttered the canvas above his head and the gulls mewed plaintively as they circled on graceful wings. But those sounds were so familiar that he was scarcely aware of them.

The hands of the old alarm clock moved slowly toward four. That would be the end of his trick, and Hoke Willens would be coming to relieve him. Barney stretched his arms and yawned. It had been a slow session. All afternoon he had logged only one Navy flying boat in addition to Slug Martin's plane. Then, all of a sudden, things began to happen.

First he saw a thread of smoke off to the south, and picked out the funnel and superstructure of a single steamer working slowly up the coast.

Then, almost at the same moment, he heard the dull thud of distant gunfire. The reports came close together—half a dozen shots—and the haze of smoke over the ship thickened to a black cloud.

Barney grabbed up the telephone. "Red flash!" he urged the operator. She must have worked fast, for he got the connection in a few seconds.

"Army emergency. Go ahead, please," said a man's voice.

"Lena Six reporting," he answered. "There's a ship being shelled by a sub. She's due south, maybe five miles, right off the inlet. Lots of smoke. Looks as if she'd been hit."

The voice at the other end was quick and tense. "One ship, five miles south of Lena Six. Shelled by sub. Probably hit. Right? Thanks!"

There was a click and the line was silent. Barney replaced the receiver and drew a long breath. He entered the report on a special sheet and clipped it to the others. It was the first time in all his months of duty that he had turned in a Red Flash message.

It was four o'clock now and Hoke Willens was usually

on time. Barney looked out and saw him coming over the top of the dune—a lean, middle-aged fisherman in flapping dungarees.

"Did ye hear the guns?" the man asked. "Looks pretty bad, way she's smokin'."

"I put in a report on her," said Barney. "You'll probably have a mess o' planes coming over pretty soon. Reckon I'll get along home an' see if Paw's going out."

He sprinted through the sand and kept on running at a jogging trot when he reached the main road. It ran down the middle of the long peninsula, the single land link between scattered settlements. Barney's house was half a mile away on the inner shore, and he was out of breath when he reached the low, weatherbeaten, gray house.

He caught a glimpse of his mother at the kitchen door, and Anna standing behind her, big-eyed and scared. The news must already have reached them.

"Where's Paw?" the boy panted.

"He and Pete went down to the dock," Mrs. Cannon answered. "They figured maybe they could help, out there."

Barney raced on till he reached the fish shed and the rickety pier that thrust out fifty feet into the sound. The *Jennie May* lay alongside, moored bow and stern to the piling, and his father and older brother were pouring gasoline from five-gallon cans into the rusty tank forward.

"You comin', too? All right, scramble aboard." It was his father who spoke. John Cannon was a big man, stoop-shouldered and powerful. There was a grim look about his gray-bristled jaws.

"Cast off," he ordered his sons. "Reckon we'll be there ahead o' the Coast Guard if we don't lose any time."

He heaved on the massive flywheel and the big two-cylinder engine broke into a throbbing roar. The *Jennie May* was a broad-beamed thirty-footer, with no beauty in her lines but staunch and seaworthy. She had a fish-well forward of the engine hatch, and her cockpit was long, wide and roomy. John Cannon spun the wheel and she chugged out into the channel and swung southward at a steady eight knots.

Pete tended the engine and Barney scrambled forward to perch on the little triangular deck in the bows. He was watching for other craft bound on the same errand as theirs, but the broad reach of water ahead was empty of boats.

One after another the channel buoys dropped astern. In a few minutes they entered the pass between their own shore and Caldee Island. Barney scowled as they came abreast of

"Caldee Castle" with its dredged and bulkheaded harbor. "You'd think some of Ohlgren's men might go out—with a boat like that," he said, jerking his thumb toward the big express cruiser moored alongside the pier.

His father and brother made no reply. There was open hostility between the longshore fishermen and the people on Caldee. It went back to the time, three years before, when the wealthy northerner, Ohlgren, had bought the sprawling, marshy island for a duck-hunting preserve. Refusing to hire any local labor, he had brought down his own carpenters and built the sumptuous, twenty-room house that he called his "shack," and the natives promptly nicknamed "the Castle." There were half a dozen servants and boatmen around the place but they were all foreigners and had little to do with folks along the sound. The only contact Barney ever had with them was when he sold fish or crabs to Kramer, the suave, cold-faced steward who managed the house.

Another mile took them out of the pass and the *Jennie May* began to pitch in the choppy seas that were racing in through the inlet. Above the noise of the waves and the engine, Barney heard another sound. It was the steady hum of airplane motors. Shading his eyes he picked out two fast-moving specks, far out over the sea. They were light bombers—A20A's, he thought—and they were roaring southward at better than 300 miles an hour.

"Must have come from way up above Edenton," he shouted back to the others. "It's been twenty minutes an' more since I phoned in the report."

The boat was past the lower end of the island now. John Cannon swung her head squarely into the breeze and she took the rough water over the bar like a bucking horse.

"Any sign o' the ship?" Pete called.

Barney stood up on the heaving bow and stared out to sea. At first all he could make out was a thin haze of smoke. Then for a moment he caught a glimpse of a dark mass, low in the water.

"Reckon that might be her," he yelled. "She's turned over, looks like. 'Bout two miles dead ahead."

A few minutes later he sang out again. "There's a raft over yonder! Look," he pointed. "Three or four men on it."

The boat veered to port and ran toward the spot. As they drew closer they could see a rubber life-raft floating high in the waves, and a number of dark heads clustered along its sides. Farther out over the ocean the bombers were circling like a pair of fish-hawks. One of them went into a sudden dive, roaring down toward the surface of the sea, then leveling out at a few hundred feet. Ten seconds later they felt the jarring thud of an exploding depth bomb.

The *Jennie May* was coming up beside the raft now, and Pete threw out the clutch so that they drifted up within arm's reach of the shipwrecked seamen. There were five of them. Four were grinning and joking as they clambered aboard. The fifth was unconscious and had to be lifted into the cockpit by two of his mates. There had been one other, they said, but he had died with a bullet through his head when the U-boat turned a machine gun on them. Their ship was the *Alissa*, a 3000-ton tramp steamer out of Havana for Baltimore with a cargo of raw sugar.

"Any more of ye afloat 'round here?" John Cannon asked.

"The mate an' most o' the rest took off in the only boat that was whole," a big, bearded sailor answered. "They'd be pretty nigh ashore by now. But there might be one or two nearer the ship."

They towed the rubber raft astern and headed out to sea once more. Another depth charge shook the boat. Barney could see the bombers still circling and diving, but the dark hulk of the *Alissa* had disappeared.

One of the survivors laughed uneasily. "Don't git too close or one o' them cans o' TNT might land on us," he said.

JENNIE MAY

"See any men swimmin'?" Barney's father called.

The boy was high on the bows again, searching the waves. At that instant a terrific explosion lifted the *Jennie May* half out of water and an enormous geyser rose out of the sea a bare two hundred yards ahead. Barney felt the deck go out from under him. Then he was plunging down through cold, green, salt water.

## 2

ARNEY was a good swimmer and his clothing—a sleeveless shirt and a pair of old dungarees—did not hamper him. But he had been thrown into the sea so suddenly there had been no time to fill his lungs with air. He fought his way to the surface sputtering and gasping. As soon as he could draw a breath and slap the water out of his eyes he looked around for the *Jennie May*.

The boat was some distance off but his father had seen him and was turning to come back. He struck out, swimming strongly, first high on the top of a wave, then deep in the trough. Suddenly, just ahead of him, a huge air bubble belched up out of the sea. There was a smell of oil and of acid. Bits of debris bobbed to the surface all around him and something white appeared, floating right in front of his face. It was a loaf of bread, wrapped in waxed paper. He laid hold of it and looked more closely. Printed on the wrapper were the words "ELIZABETH CITY BAKERY—Whole milk bread, enriched with Vitamin B—Elizabeth City, N. C."

At that moment the *Jennie May's* bow swung past and Pete reached out an arm to him. Still clutching the loaf of bread, he was pulled in over the side and joined the dripping men in the cockpit.

"What in tarnation ye got there?" his father asked. "Bread? It'll be spoilt, floatin' 'round in the ocean all that time."

Barney laid the loaf on the seat beside him and carefully opened one end of the wrapper. Aside from the moisture from his fingers the bread inside was dry and in good condition.

"Well, I'll be purely switched!" John Cannon muttered. "Where'd it come from?"

"You can see it hadn't been in the water but a couple o' minutes," said Barney. "So there's only two places it could ha' come from—the ship or the submarine. An' look at the name on the wrapper!"

His father stared at the printing. "You fellers come here straight from Havana?" he asked the bearded seaman.

"Sure did. We was two weeks in port, loadin' cargo, an'

come up from Rio before that."

He looked about for corroboration and his companions nodded.

Barney's father poked at the bread with a huge forefinger. "Think that last bomb got the U-boat?" he asked. "There don't seem to be much of an oil slick."

"No," said the boy. "But I think they got her just the same." He mentioned the big air bubble and the strange smells. "An' this bread," he added. "How else did it come here? Somebody's been getting supplies out to the Germans —somebody right along this coast!"

There was silence in the boat. Each man was thinking his own grim thoughts as the *Jennie May* headed homeward. The two bombers were vanishing specks far to the north, but a Coast Guard patrol boat was coming down the shore. She intercepted them a mile from the mouth of the inlet and lay to while the survivors of the *Alissa* were transferred.

She was a fast ninety-footer in gray war paint, and she had torpedo tubes and a three-inch gun mounted forward. Barney knew one or two men in her crew.

"Reckon they got the sub," he shouted to the gunner's mate who leaned over the side. "There was one depth charge nearly wrecked us, an' right afterward a lot of oil an' stuff came up."

The Coast Guard sailor grinned. "They let it go some-times, just to fool us," he said. "I don't claim any sinkings unless I plant a shell square in the conning tower. An' even then I like to see a couple o' dead Jerries before I'm con-vinced."

Barney laughed. "You're hard to please," he replied. "Maybe if you'd been swimming 'round in it, like I was, you'd think different."

As soon as the five sailors and their raft were aboard, the patrol boat roared away to reconnoiter the scene of the sink-ing and look for other possible survivors. The *Jennie May* chugged on into the sound. John Cannon and his boys weren't given to much talking. They were nearing their home dock before the father spoke. "Sort o' shot the after-noon to pieces," he remarked, spitting over the side. "But I reckon maybe 'twas worth it."

*　　*　　*

There were fish to be cleaned from the morning's catch, and Barney helped Pete with the work until suppertime. Hoke Willens dropped in as they were getting up from the table and reported that the *Alissa's* lifeboat, with sixteen men, had landed a short distance from the lookout post. He had telephoned a Red Flash message and the Coast Guard truck had come down to pick them up.

Barney gave Anna a hand with the dishes. She was pale and he could see she had been crying. Her own terrible experience was still fresh in her memory, and a sea tragedy brought it back in all its frightfulness. She had seen her mother drown.

The boy patted her shoulder in an awkward attempt to comfort her. "I'd stay an' play dominoes with you," he told her, "but I've got to go up the beach tonight. It's something important, I reckon."

He changed to clean trousers and shirt and went out to the lean-to shed that served as a stable. His pony whinnied softly as he went into the stall beside her. Judy was one of the tough, wiry little horses that run wild on some of the coastal islands. He had broken her to ride when he was twelve, and she could still carry him easily, though he was a big, rangy boy for his age. He rode bareback and used only a rope hackamore to guide her.

In a few minutes they were moving north along the sandy road at Judy's quick trot. She tossed her head and snorted two or three times as the salty evening breeze came over the dunes.

Under his arm Barney carried the loaf of bread he had salvaged from the sea. He didn't know just what its significance was, but he meant to find out.

His destination was the small Army airfield where Slug Martin's observation unit was based. The runways were laid out in the flat country behind the dunes and the hangars were dug out of the dunes themselves and cleverly hidden under sand and grass.

Three miles up the road, Barney came to a barbed wire fence where a khaki-clad sentry challenged him. The boy had been there often before, and the soldier recognized his face.

"You want to see Lieutenant Martin, huh? Well, I got orders not to let any civilians through, but you're on the lookout post. Sort of attached to the Fighter Command. That might make it all right. You better wait till my relief comes, though, an' I'll go in with you."

Barney tethered his pony to the fence and chatted with the sentry for ten minutes. Then another man came tramping out of the dusk and took over the guard duty. Accompanied by the first soldier, Barney went on a few hundred yards to the huddle of fishermen's houses that had been taken over as barracks and officers' quarters.

Three or four young fliers were sitting outside the largest building, enjoying the cool of the evening, and the boy heard Slug Martin's Texas drawl among their voices. As he came closer the pilot unfolded his lanky six-foot frame and held out a hand.

"Doggone," he chuckled. "My ol' fishin' pardner, Barney Cannon. Hiya, son?"

"Hi, yourself," Barney grinned. "Saw you go over, this noontime. But where were you when the real fuss started?"

"Me an' my little bus were makin' a three-point landin' back here about that time. You had a chance to report it, didn't you?"

"Yep. An' I was out there with Paw, hauling out survivors, when they got the U-boat."

The tall Texan whistled. "Think they got her? The bomber boys weren't kiddin', then."

"Here's why I think so," Barney said, holding out the loaf of bread.

They went inside to Martin's room, and there the boy told him the whole story. "Of course," he finished, "they might have let some oil an' pieces o' wreckage go just to fool us, like the gunner said. But this bread is something they'd want to keep mum about. It's a give-away. It means they're getting supplies from the mainland!"

Martin took the loaf out of the wrapper and cut into it carefully with his pocket-knife.

"Fresh enough to eat," he said. "Can't be more'n three days old. That's a queer one, sure 'nough. I always said you fishermen were an ornery bunch. But givin' aid an' comfort to the enemy? No—I wouldn't have believed it!"

"This was no fisherman," Barney replied with heat. "I know 'em all. Some are cranky an' some are mean, but they all hate Germans. Why, they even wanted to have us send little Anna to a concentration camp till Paw put his foot down."

The pilot nodded. "Just the same," he said, "somebody must be doing it, an' we'd better find out who in a hurry. If they can get fresh bread they can get fresh news—ship news. S'pose you leave this with me, Barney, an' let me talk to my C.O. He'll likely want to call Intelligence about it. If they need to see you, I'll send you word. Got any ideas, yourself?"

"About the bread, you mean? Well, if they could trace it from the bakery to folks that bought it—but that's impossible. Their trucks go all over this part o' the country, an' their bread's sold in a lot o' stores besides. Well, I'll keep puzzling at it. Maybe a hunch'll come to me."

"So long, now," Martin grinned. "Don't land with your wheels up!"

Barney did plenty of speculating on the ride home, but somehow his thoughts always came back to the same place—Caldee Island. The activities of most of the coast people were well known to their neighbors, but what might go on at the big hunting lodge nobody knew. It had only been the previous autumn that one of the Willens boys was shot at, when he rowed his boat into a tide creek down there, looking for crabs. Kramer had apologized afterward, and sent out word that he'd fired the man, but he let it be known that Ohlgren had given him strict orders to keep poachers off the island.

"Poachers!" That was a word that rubbed all the free and easy longshore people the wrong way. Maybe it was right for the government to put a law on duck-shooting, but in open season a fellow ought to be able to take his gun where he liked.

There were ways, though, in which Barney could visit the island without getting into trouble. They liked good food at Caldee, and Kramer would pay well for a mess of fresh-caught spots or other pan fish.

He had his plan worked out before he fell asleep that night. In the morning he was out before daylight in the skiff, and by the time the sun was well up and he was really hungry he had a fair-sized catch of silvery fish squirming and flopping in the bottom of the boat.

Anna met him at the dock. "Why didn't you wait for me, Barney?" she pouted. "I love to fish. But you had good luck, no? Maybe I cook some of them for your breakfast."

"Not these," he told her. "I've got a special use for 'em. I'll take you next time, though."

He threw some wet seaweed over the fish in the boat and went to the house. As soon as he had eaten he rowed out into the channel and headed south for Caldee. It was hot. The waters of the sound were calm under a sultry sun. Barney pulled off his shirt, and his body, naked above the waist, was as brown as an Indian's. He pulled steadily, with quick, short, fisherman's strokes, and the light skiff moved swiftly south into the pass.

When he rounded the bulkhead and headed into the narrow harbor he could see that the big motorboat was not at her mooring. There was nobody in sight on the shore. The low, white buildings glared under the brassy sun and no breeze stirred the carefully planted shrubbery at the corners of the wide veranda.

In a silence that was almost sinister, Barney tied his painter to the dock and climbed the ladder. His bare feet padded on the gravel path as he circled the house to reach the kitchen door. He heard voices coming from the windows at the rear. They were men's voices, speaking in guttural German.

"*Sehr heiss*," one of them grumbled. "Very hot." And he went on to say he wouldn't have come here, even at Ohlgren's wages, if he had known he was going to fry all day.

Barney knocked at the screen door and there was sudden quiet inside. After a moment he heard the sound of rubber-soled shoes, and Kramer appeared. He was a powerfully built man of thirty-five or forty, thin-lipped and strong-jawed. Close-cropped light brown hair stood in a stiff brush above his pale face. His narrow gray-blue eyes were cold as ice.

"Yes?" he said, after a long scrutiny of Barney's face. "You are the boy who sells fish, not?"

"That's right," Barney answered. "I've got a nice mess o' spots, just caught this morning."

"So?" There was no telling, from the softly spoken word or from the man's face, whether he was interested in fish or not. Behind his impassive scrutiny he seemed to be thinking of something else.

At last he nodded. "Very good," he said. "I will look at them."

He vanished for a moment, then came back with a large market basket. Together they went around to the dock.

The spots were still moist and fresh under the covering of seaweed. Kramer felt of them judicially and appeared to be satisfied. "How much for the lot?" he asked.

"A dollar ought to be enough," said Barney. "There's better'n twenty pounds there. Can you folks eat 'em all? Or maybe Mr. Ohlgren's bringing down a party."

Kramer looked at him with a quick frown. "We are always ready for Mr. Ohlgren's guests," he said evenly. "As for his plans, they are his own affair."

There was a chilling finality about those last words that warned Barney against any further prying. He dropped his eyes and began filling the basket with fish. Kramer walked back to the house and the boy followed. At the kitchen door he handed the basket over and Kramer gave him a dollar bill. The silence had become oppressive.

"If you should want some more," Barney mumbled, "or some crabs or something—I'll be glad to bring 'em over."

Kramer's nod was non-committal. He closed the door and

the boy was left standing there, a flush creeping up under his tan. He turned and went back to the boat. In his heart, as he rowed out into the pass, was a strange mixture of anger and cold, nameless dread.

**3**

THE work of pulling the oars in the blazing heat soon restored Barney's balance. He'd been imagining things, he told himself. Kramer was a mean customer, sure, but maybe that was just because he was a northerner. Only he didn't talk like a Yankee. His accent was foreign. And they spoke German in the Castle kitchen. Still, the words he had heard were innocent enough.

The tide, which had helped him on his way down, was still running out strongly through the pass, and it was hard to make any headway. After twenty minutes of heavy rowing Barney decided to pull in along the shore and wait for the turn of the tide. He was a good half mile above the entrance to the harbor, and he doubted if any guards would be posted on the marsh in such scorching weather. As he came opposite the mouth of a little tidal creek he swung the bow in and came to rest by a mud-flat in the tall reeds.

Two or three gulls rose and flew in wide circles, their cries sometimes plaintive, sometimes like jeering laughter. He sat still in the boat and they soon forgot his presence. The other marsh birds went about their business. A broad-winged fish-hawk soared high above the channel. Snipe ran daintily along the muddy shore, picking at the tiny shellfish that lay exposed by the low tide.

Barney watched the water and saw that it was no longer running toward the sea. Just as he decided the slack had come and was about to grasp the oars, a deep, throbbing hum reached his ears. He glanced upward but there was no plane in the sky. The sound was made by the engines of a big motorboat, and it was coming fast.

The boy stood up cautiously. He could just see over the tops of the reeds without himself being seen. In a moment Ohlgren's cruiser came into view. She was tearing along at twenty knots, so close to the shore that Barney could have hit her with a stone. He saw sailors' white uniforms and the glitter of brasswork. Across her broad stern was her name, in big, shining letters—"VALKYR."

It was a funny name for a boat, he thought. Maybe it was a girl's name in some foreign lingo. He'd have to ask Anna about it.

He pushed off with an oar and watched the cruiser as she approached the bulkhead at the harbor entrance. But instead of cutting her motors and turning in she roared on, heading down the pass toward the inlet. If she had been up to Manteo Island for provisions it was queer that she didn't take them to the Castle. Maybe Ohlgren had a fishing party aboard. He wondered if the big motorboat had a permit to go outside. Probably a rich man like Ohlgren would manage to get one, even when the government was so strict with the ordinary fishermen.

With the help of the incoming tide he made good time on the row back, and arrived just as his mother was clearing away the dinner dishes.

"I saved some for you," she said. "Sit down an' I'll get it out o' the oven. Where you been all morning?"

"Took a load o' spots down to Caldee," he replied casually. "Got a dollar for 'em. Here 'tis." And he gave her the bill.

"Good," she said. "They're not much as neighbors, but they spend their money. I'll put this toward a pair o' winter shoes for you. You better stay 'round. The boat'll be back in another hour or two an' I reckon they'll have some fish to clean."

It wasn't until that evening that he had a chance to talk to Anna. "Ever hear of a name spelled v-a-l-k-y-r?" he asked her.

She spelled it over to herself and her face brightened. "Ach, yes," she said. "In Wagner's operas of the Ring. The Valkyrie were women—well, like women, but like gods, too. They rode on wild horses in the air over the battlefields, and they carried off the dying heroes to Valhalla—what you say —heaven. That is very German, that name."

"Hm! Yeah," said Barney. "I figured maybe it was. It's the name on Ohlgren's boat. He seems to run to Germans, round his place, though folks say he's a Swede."

"That would be all right," Anna nodded, and she tried to explain how Scandinavian and German mythology were interwoven.

"Maybe so," the boy agreed. "But Kramer's a Nazi, I'd take a bet. An' I heard some other men talking German down there."

The girl's blue eyes grew wide with fright. "A Nazi— here?" she whispered. "Oh—that is bad!"

"Listen," said Barney. "You can keep a secret, Anna, an' I'm going to trust you. Promise you won't say a word about it, even to Maw?"

She promised and there was no mistaking the fact that she meant it. Barney told her all he knew or suspected. It was a relief to have someone at home in whom he could confide. She was very quiet while he talked, but he could see she was thinking.

"That is how they work, the Nazis," she said when he finished. "They have secret friends helping them everywhere. But in this peaceful place I hoped it would be different. Oh, we must do something, Barney! The police—the soldiers—somebody must be told."

The boy was doubtful. "They wouldn't take much stock in it, I'm 'fraid," he told her. "Still, Slug Martin's getting Army Intelligence to work on that bread business. Maybe I'll have a chance to tell 'em about Caldee."

Barney hung around the house and the dock next morning, hoping for some word from his pilot friend. But none had come when he left for the lookout post a little before noon. The sky was overcast and a shift in the wind to the northward warned of unsettled weather. The air was much cooler than the day before.

Evan Blake was standing on top of the dune beside the shelter. "Looks like some fresh wreckage down the beach there a ways," he pointed. "Now you're here I'll go an' have a look."

Barney took his place under the canvas and watched the other lad stride down the sand. The coast for fifty miles north of Hatteras was strewn with wrecks and driftwood. Some of the hulks had been imbedded in the beach for generations. What Blake had seen was a smaller object, washed in by the last tide. He stooped above it, then picked it up and carried it toward the shelter.

"What you got?" Barney called.

"Looks like some sort of a camp chair. It's busted, though."

He scrambled up the dune and laid the thing down in front of Barney. It was, as he had said, a folding chair, made of light, gray-painted wood and white canvas. One of the legs was broken. Barney lifted the chair and turned it over and both boys stared in sudden wonder. On the back of the canvas was painted a black and yellow hornet, and below it, on a round, red background, was the unmistakable shape of a black swastika.

"Gosh!" breathed Blake. "German!"

"Sure is," said Barney. "It's off that sub the bombers got, day before yesterday. They paint pictures of animals an' things on their conning towers an' other places. Remember, last year, when the sailors off a couple o' ships that were sunk told about a laughing cow painted on the U-boat that got 'em? This is the same idea. A hornet, see? Maybe the chair was in the skipper's cabin. Well, this is one hornet that won't sting any more!"

Blake nodded, open-mouthed. "Durned if I don't b'lieve you're right," he said. "Know what I'm goin' to do? I bet the beach patrol ought to see this. I'll take it on up a ways an' meet 'em."

"You don't need to," Barney told him, looking north along the dune. "I can see 'em now."

Sure enough, a pair of Coast Guard sailors were in sight, coming along the sand. One carried a rifle slung at his back, and a big Navy pistol hung from the other's belt. They paced along in stride, silent because everything they had to say to each other had long since been said.

Evan called to them and the two men climbed the dune to see what he had found. After one glimpse of the design on the chair-back the sailor with the rifle whistled. "Guess that sort o' proves something, don't it?" he asked his mate. "Maybe those Army bombers did it, after all."

"Yep," said the other. "We'd better take it up to the station. Where'd you pick it up, Buddy?"

Blake showed them the spot, below the tide line. "I know 'twasn't here yesterday," he told them, "because I was by here two-three times. Must ha' washed in this mornin'."

The Coast Guard men went on down the beach, leaving the chair to be picked up on their return, and Blake went home to dinner. Alone in the shelter, Barney turned once more to the monotonous task of watching sea and sky. He had eaten something before he left the house. This time Anna would not be bringing him his lunch, and a lonely afternoon stretched before him.

Slug Martin was late today. It was after one o'clock before the distant hum of his plane gave the boy an opportunity to pick up the telephone. He was just finishing the call when he saw the low-flying plane circle over the beach and head back toward his post. Then something dropped from the cockpit, and an instant later a long yellow streamer unfolded, fluttering slowly downward. Martin banked again, dipped a wing in salute and sailed off over the sea.

There was a small khaki-colored object attached to the yellow tail. Barney jumped out of the shelter and ran down the dune, reaching the flat cloth packet almost as soon as it touched the sand. It was of waterproof material, a few inches square. He unsnapped the flap and opened it. Inside was a folded sheet of notepaper, addressed with a flourish to "Barney Cannon, Esq."

The message was brief but it made the boy's pulse beat faster.

"Have talked to the C.O. and shown him your find. He took it up with the proper parties and they're making an investigation. Haven't said anything about this, but just on a hunch you might keep an eye on Caldee after dark. Better destroy this. Bring chute back to me when you've got anything to report. Happy landings! Slug."

Barney burned the note and folded the streamer and packet into a neat bundle. It gave him a thrill to know that the pilot shared his feeling about the people on Caldee. But "after dark" meant a different kind of scouting than merely selling fish at the back door. He would have to go alone and make some excuse to the family, for he was pretty sure his father would forbid such an expedition if he knew about it.

It was a long wait till four o'clock. As soon as his relief arrived he went home and got the small flashlight that hung on a nail between his bed and his brother's. Nobody saw him as he carried it down to the dock and stowed it under a thwart in the rowboat. The *Jennie May* came in a few minutes later, and he was busy helping clean the catch until suppertime.

At the table he told the story of the folding chair Blake had found on the beach. Pete had heard about the animal emblems used by German submarines and had no doubt the hornet was one of them. "I was plenty sure in my own mind she was hit," he said. "An' this looks like proof. You say the patrol took it? Reckon I'll ramble up to the station tonight. Maybe I can get to see it."

Barney was afraid for a minute that his brother would want the boat, but he set off on foot. There was a girl who lived a mile up the road, and Pete would probably make a little call there on the way.

After a few minutes Barney rose and stretched. "Thought I might row up to Evan's for a while," he explained casually. "He may want me to help him work on his boat. Don't worry about me if I don't get in till late."

His father looked at him but made no comment. Mrs. Cannon was out of the room, and if Anna suspected something, she kept it to herself. He sauntered down to the dock and got into the boat. In order not to be a liar he rowed north a half mile to the Blakes' landing, talked to Evan for a little while, and gave him a hand with the skiff he was building. When dusk fell he pushed off again and started rowing down the sound. The tide was on the ebb and the boat bobbed along swiftly in the current. He was well out from shore when he passed the home dock, and he didn't think he could be seen in the gathering dark.

The night was overcast and without stars. A light, uncertain wind from the east blew in across the dunes and raised a chop in the channel. But Barney knew those waters like the back of his hand. He pulled over to the right as he neared Caldee, and skirted the reedy shore more by feel than by sight.

Just north of the entrance to the Castle's little harbor, he waited, resting on his oars and listening. There was no sound but the lap of waves among the reeds and the sleepy squawk of a nesting gull. Barney shipped one oar silently and poled in with the other till the flat bow grounded on the mud. His heart was beating fast as he stepped ashore. He knew little about the habits of these strange people, but he was pretty certain they kept some sort of watch against snoopers.

Bent low, he crept forward through the tall, rustling reeds till he could feel the timbers of the bulkhead under his toes and see the faint shimmer of water in the harbor. Where he stood, he was less than a hundred yards from the dock.

Again he waited and listened. This time he heard something—a steady, muffled chugging of powerful motors, throttled down. A boat was coming up the pass toward the harbor mouth. Barney ducked back into the reeds and worked his way westward, in the direction of the house. He had gone only a short distance when the sound of motors came from right abreast of him. Crouching, he edged over to the bulkhead and peered out at the passing craft.

It was Ohlgren's big cruiser, slipping in at two or three knots, and showing no lights except a hooded spotlight mounted on the streamlined pilot-house. Its narrow beam played restlessly along the shore and the dock, and in that sharply focused glare the boy saw three figures running down to the landing.

Someone aboard the boat asked a low-voiced question. There were respectful answers, and a command of some kind, in German, which Barney could not catch. The craft was nosing smoothly in along the pier. A thrown rope was caught and made fast. Then, to the boy's amazement, the men on the dock snapped to rigid attention, heads back, hands stiffly at their sides. And just as the spotlight was turned off he saw—or thought he saw—two figures in white naval uniform step from the deck to the pier.

# 4

CALDEE CASTLE itself was built on filled land that had been dredged out of the harbor basin. The ground near the house was graded and covered by a smoothly trimmed lawn, well above the level of the surrounding marsh. Except for some planted shrubbery, flanking the veranda, there was no cover for anyone who wanted to approach unseen.

As soon as the single light aboard the *Valkyr* was switched off, the basin and dock were plunged into total darkness. Barney hesitated a second, then stole along the bulkhead toward the house as rapidly as he could move without making a noise. There were soft lights glowing behind the venetian blinds at two of the windows, and the front door was standing ajar. The boy stopped when he reached the edge of the cleared ground, but he was near enough now to command a view of the steps and the entrance.

The people from the boat were walking up the path. In the lead were three figures, more distinct as they drew closer to the light. One was a tall, heavy man in dark coat, white trousers and yachting cap—Mr. Ohlgren, himself, Barney thought. Beside him marched the two men in uniform, their erect, military bearing in sharp contrast to his slouching bulk. They were talking in low tones, but the crunch of the gravel under their feet blurred the sound so that the boy was unable to catch any words.

At the threshold the big man stood aside to let his guests pass in first, and then the door closed behind the three of them. The rest of the party went along the path and on to the rear of the building.

Barney waited till he heard the back door slam before he drew a long breath. He brushed away the mosquitoes that had settled on his bare arms and neck. Their bites made little impression on his toughened hide. What he minded more was a tingly feeling down his spine—a warning through all his senses that after what he had seen it was time to get out of there in a hurry. He slipped back once more into the reeds and silently retraced his steps to the boat.

He had to heave to get her off, for the tide had gone down several inches while he was ashore. At first it was heavy rowing against the current. But soon the ebb began to slacken and he was able to make some headway. He pulled over to the east side of the pass, first to get as far from the forbidding island as he could, and second to reach the lee of the dunes, where the waves were less choppy. He had left Caldee well astern and was rowing up the channel a mile below the home landing when he heard a hail from shore.

It was a girl's voice, high-pitched and clear. "Oh, Barney!"

He rested on his oars and shouted back. "That you, Anna?"

"Yes," she called. "Can you come and get me?"

He pulled around with his right oar and headed in her direction. The shore was sandy and shelving at that point and the girl had no trouble scrambling into the boat. When she was sitting in the stern-sheets, facing him, he started north again without a word.

After a minute or two she broke the silence. "I suppose it was wrong of me to follow you." Her voice sounded small and unhappy.

"I like folks to mind their own business," he replied.

"Yes," she said. "But, Barney, I was afraid. I guessed where you were going."

The boy relented somewhat after that. "All right," he said. "But doggone it, you shouldn't have come. Maw'll be wondering where you've been, an' I don't want to have to explain."

"You—you went there again?" Anna whispered. "Did they see you?"

"Not me. I saw them, though. You know that boat I was telling about—the *Valkyr?* She came in without running lights. Had what looked like a couple o' Navy big shots aboard."

"Navy?" asked the girl. "What Navy?"

"That's what I'd like to know," Barney muttered. "There was something funny about those uniforms. They didn't look just right."

Anna's face was only a pale oval in the darkness, but he could see the frightened quiver of her shoulders.

"I must be cold," she said. "The night air—"

"Now look here," he told her. "Don't you go an' get upset. I reckon I've imagined most of it, an' anyhow nobody's going to do anything to you. Far as I'm concerned, you don't have to worry about me, either. I can take care o' myself."

There was a light still burning in the house when they

landed. Mrs. Cannon sat by the table, darning socks.

"Well!" she said. "I was starting to fidget. Where did you two go to?"

Barney grinned. "You get excited easy, Maw," he answered. "I told 'em at supper where I was going—up to Evan Blake's. Anna was taking a walk alongshore. I picked her up on my way home."

"All right," Mrs. Cannon nodded. "Better get to bed now. I s'pose Pete'll be out till all hours, but I don't want your father waked up."

She reached up to rumple her boy's hair and gave Anna an affectionate pat on the arm as she passed. They said goodnight and went to their rooms.

As he crawled into bed, Barney had a guilty feeling. He hadn't told his mother the whole truth. The only excuse he could offer his conscience was that the good woman would have lain awake worrying if she had known. But beyond that he wanted to be free to go again to Caldee. He had what amounted to an order from the Army to keep an eye on the place, and now he felt surer than ever that it would bear watching. Before sleep overtook him he made a firm resolve to see Slug Martin in the morning.

*　　*　　*

Barney crept out of bed at the earliest crack of dawn. He left Pete sleeping heavily in the other cot, got himself a bite of breakfast and fed and watered Judy. When she had finished her hay he mounted and rode northward.

There was no sun that morning. By the time he reached the airfield fence a steady, light drizzle was falling from the gray sky. This time the sentry on duty was a friend of his and passed him through.

A company of enlisted men was drawn up in the rain in front of the barracks doing calisthenic drill. As the sergeant yelped a series of unintelligible orders the men bent from the waist, jumped or flexed their arms in unison. Watching them, Barney waited by the door of Slug Martin's quarters till a young pilot officer came out. He was wearing bathing trunks and carried a towel over his shoulder.

"Lieutenant Martin?" he answered the boy. "Sure, he'll be along in a minute. We're goin' for a swim in the sound before breakfast."

Slug appeared presently, his lean, wiry body brown from the sun. He greeted Barney with a slap on the back. "Come on down with me," he urged. "You don't need a bathin' suit. There's no women around."

After he had returned the packet that had held the message, the boy accompanied his friend down to the shore. There was a diving-board rigged up there, and for ten minutes they plunged and splashed like a pair of retriever pups.

The other airman had gone back to the house when they came out and toweled themselves. Martin glanced up and down the shore to make certain there was nobody else within earshot.

"I sort o' think we were on the right track," he said. "The skipper got some news last night. Intelligence has been lookin' around in the stores up the sound. They couldn't trace your loaf o' bread but they found out somethin' else. That man Kramer at Caldee has been buyin' mighty heavy on some kinds o' groceries. Before the sugar rationin' started he laid in five barrels. Then he got half a dozen sides o' bacon an' three or four hundred pounds o' butter at one crack. You might think he figured no more butter was goin' to be made for the duration! How many men you reckon there are to feed, down at the island?"

"With the regular help, not more'n six or eight," Barney guessed. "Come duck season they sometimes have big parties there, but that's three months off. Now I've got some news o' my own."

While he pulled on his damp clothes he told Martin about

his two trips to Caldee. When he described the guests who had landed from the cruiser, his friend's eyes narrowed and he gave a low whistle.

"Man, oh, man!" he breathed. "An' you say those Heinies on the dock stood at attention? Hmm! Could be, I s'pose, that they were officers off one of our coast patrol ships. But doggone it, why did the boat sneak in that way—showin' no lights?"

He was still mulling over Barney's story as they walked up to the quarters. "I'd tell the C.O. about this in a minute," he said. "Trouble is he's gone to Norfolk an' won't be back till this evenin'. What I'd like to know is whether the cruiser's still tied up at the island. If she is, I reckon the visitors are there, too. Tell you what—I'll fly down that way this noon. You be watchin' for me, an' when I come back over your place I'll cut the motor two-three times if the boat's moored at the dock. If she's gone, I'll just pass right over with no signal. Then you'll know whether it's worth your while to make another trip down there tonight. I'd say you might see somethin' if those white uniforms are still around."

"I don't know as I can make it," Barney replied. "But I'll do my darnedest. This is my day off at the lookout, so I'll be somewhere 'round the house or the dock when you come over. I sure wish your major was here. Maybe we could get some quick action."

"Yeah, I know. I'd talk to the officer in charge, only he hasn't been in on this an' I don't think the skipper would like it. So if I give you the signal you try to see an' hear all you can. If there's anything to our hunch, you can bet the Army'll step on that gang pronto."

Barney reached home a half hour later and found he was in time to do the morning chores around the house and dock. When his father asked where he had been, he told him. John Cannon had no objection to his friendship with the young pilot. In fact he had given Barney silent encouragement when he announced his intention of enlisting in the Air Force as soon as he was old enough.

"Sort of a wet mornin' for a swim, wasn't it?" the older man remarked drily. "Well, everybody to his own taste. You go help Pete with the fish. An' 'fore we start out you'd better pump the rain water out o' the *Jennie May*."

The Cannons' gasoline was rationed, like everyone else's along the Eastern seaboard. And even though working boats were allowed more than pleasure craft, they had to be careful not to waste it. For that reason they always timed their fishing trips with the tide.

"Ebb's still runnin'," Pete told his brother after a glance at the current passing the pier. "She'll start to turn about eleven, so you better get busy with the bilge pump."

Barney spent the next fifteen minutes working the wooden plunger up and down and watching the water slowly disappear from the boat's bottom. He was just finishing when his father came down the dock.

"We're goin' to need a spare hand, today," he told the boy. "Want you to come along. You all ready?"

Barney's heart sank. If he went out with the boat he wouldn't be on hand to catch Martin's signal. But John Cannon was no man to argue with.

"Be ready in a minute," he answered, stowing the pump under a thwart. "I've got to go up to the house first."

He found Anna peeling potatoes in the kitchen. Fortunately she was alone, and he told her his predicament as quickly as he could.

"So I reckon it's up to you," he finished. "He'll be over sometime around noon, an' you'll have to listen to the noise his engine makes. Then tell me when I get back."

She nodded, her blue eyes scared and solemn. Barney grabbed a slicker from the row of hooks in the shed and hurried back in time to swing aboard the *Jennie May* as she cast off.

There was little wind that day, and the steady, light rain flattened the waves outside. They lay at anchor, three or four miles offshore, and fished with handlines while the boat lifted and settled to the long ground swell. It was monotonous work but they got a fair catch of fish.

Barney, ravenous after his early breakfast, was glad when his father opened the lunch-box and doled out sandwiches. It was close to four o'clock when the anchor was hauled up and Pete started the engine. They ran in on the last of the flood tide and were moored to the dock by five.

With the unloading and cleaning up it was suppertime before Barney had an opportunity to see Anna. The others had gone in ahead of him and he was hanging up his wet rain-clothes in the shed when she stole out to meet him.

"The airplane made a signal," she whispered. "It flew very low and your mother was afraid. Then the engine stopped—*brrrp*—*brrrp*—like so!"

Barney looked at her. "Okay, Anna," he said. "That means I've got to go again tonight. I won't have any excuse this time, so I'll just sneak out. An' you won't know anything about it if they ask. Promise?"

She nodded, her lips trembling and her eyes close to tears.

"Please, Barney—please be careful," she whispered, as they started toward the kitchen.

The boy washed his face and hands at the sink and sat down to supper. It was a good meal, but he was unable either to eat very heartily or to share in the conversation. A nervous excitement made him fidgety. When Pete and his father settled down to a game of checkers he got out his well-worn copy of a book on fighting planes and tried to read. As soon as it was dark outside he laid the book down, stretched and yawned, and went casually out the back door as if he meant to look at the weather. Two minutes later he was rowing quietly away from the dock in the rain.

5

BARNEY had never been out on the sound on a darker night. By the time he figured he was in the pass abreast of Caldee he could barely see the stern of his own boat. He pulled cautiously over to the westward and knew he was close to the land because he could catch the pungent, salty smell of the tide flats. After a moment he reached out his hand and felt the tall reeds, close to the gunwale. Once or twice, as he worked the boat slowly southward, the flat bottom scraped on the mud.

At last he came to the place where he had beached the skiff the night before. He ran it in as far as it would go, then pulled the bow still higher to make sure it would stay there till he returned.

Foot by foot, he felt his way toward the edge of the basin. He had come out without a slicker and the drizzle had soaked

58

him to the skin. But it was not the chill of the rain that made him shiver. A sixth sense told him that tonight he was running into real danger.

When he finally found the bulkhead he waited long minutes, listening. There was no sound except the drip and rustle of raindrops in the reeds, and the gurgle of water around the heavy timbers. The dock lay in pitchy blackness, but a dim halo of light could be seen around the front windows of the Castle.

He stayed there long enough to make certain that nobody was on the bulkhead between him and the house. Then he began moving very slowly toward those rain-blurred lights.

At the edge of the lawn he crouched low and waited again. It was tantalizing to be so near and yet have no opportunity to see or hear anything. The slats of the blinds were drawn tight, but a faint murmur of voices reached him. Some of the windows must be open. After several minutes of shivering discomfort, he grew reckless. If he didn't want to go home without getting any information he must cross the thirty yards of dark lawn to the nearest corner of the building. He had watched carefully and there had been no sign of a sentry or a moving figure since his arrival. He wondered about that. It might mean one of two things. Either his whole theory was wrong and they had no secrets to guard, or the men assigned to the job had gone inside out of the weather.

Barney was too cold and miserable to stay where he was. He screwed up his courage at last and darted across the open space as fast as his numb legs could take him. There was a clump of small, bushy evergreens at the side of the porch near one of the windows, and it was toward that shelter that he raced.

He was panting and his heart pounded with excitement as he crept into the protecting shrubbery. It took a moment or two for him to get settled in his listening-post and concentrate on the voices that came through the window. Some one was telling a story in German. He couldn't catch enough words to keep the thread of the narrative but there must have been something funny about it. At the end he heard subdued laughter and a few chuckles.

Then a high, metallic voice gave a command. "More schnapps, Fritz." There was a sound of pouring from a bottle, a hiss of seltzer and a tinkle of ice. The same voice that had ordered the liquor was raised again in sharp authority: "*Heil Hitler!*"

"*Heil Hitler!*" two voices answered. One was a deep rumble, the other cold and colorless.

"To a successful voyage!" the first man spoke once more, and again his companions echoed the toast.

Barney held his breath. This was all the proof of treachery that he could ask—far more than he had looked for. Now it was time to act. He was on his hands and knees, half-way out of his shelter when he heard a quick patter of feet.

It was too late to scramble back. Before he could make a move there was a hoarse growl a few yards away, and then a huge, black shape launched itself at him. Barney flung himself on his back, defending himself, with knees and arms. But the giant police dog did not touch him. It stood there just over him with bared fangs, the terrible growl rolling like thunder in its throat.

The dog lifted its head and barked twice. And almost instantly there was a sound of feet pounding along the path. The next thing Barney knew, he was being jerked upright by strong, ruthless hands. Two men gripped him by the arms. They were panting and cursing under their breath as they hurried him along the gravel to the back door. The glare of lights in the kitchen blinded him for a moment and he blinked uncertainly. Then a stinging slap across his face rocked his head back.

In front of him stood Kramer, staring at him with stony

eyes.

"So-o," the steward murmured and licked his thin lips. "It is you, my inquisitive young friend. And I suppose you have come to sell some fish or crabs—no? That is too bad—for you. It seems you came at the wrong time!"

Kramer turned suddenly to one of the boy's captors. "Where was he, Rudel?" he snarled in German.

"Under the bush, close to the window," the man replied.

"Leave him here and go—quickly!" Kramer shouted. "There may be others. Search the grounds and the shore. No spies must get away!"

He grasped Barney by the collar of his wet shirt as the two others hurried out into the night. Just then the door at the opposite side of the room swung open. A scared-looking young man in a white waiter's jacket stood there. "They—they want to know what is the trouble," he stammered.

Kramer scowled. "Nothing, Fritz," he said. "Tell them nothing at all. The dog barked at a rat"—he gave Barney a shake—"but we have caught it."

The servant started to go back, but he had taken only a step when a bulky figure loomed in the doorway. Barney knew it was the owner of Caldee Island. The man had a broad, pale face with little, pig-like eyes and a spiky blond ıustache. The light gleamed on his bald head, set low between hulking shoulders. He still wore the blue yachting coat and white trousers the boy had seen the night before.

Ohlgren strode ponderously into the kitchen, a scowl wrinkling his forehead. "*Was ist los?*" he snapped. "What's wrong?"

It was Kramer's turn to be uncomfortable. "This boy," he replied in German. "We found him hiding in the bushes near the house." He hauled Barney forward by the collar.

"Who is he?"

"Son of a fisherman—from one of those shanties across the channel. He has been here before, selling fish."

A surge of anger reddened Ohlgren's unhealthy face. He bent his head and glared into Barney's eyes. "*Versteh'n Sie Deutsch?*" he barked.

The boy knew well enough that he was being asked if he understood German. Fortunately he was too scared to open his mouth in answer. He merely blinked and tried to look as stupid as possible.

"It's not likely," Kramer put in, recovering some of his suavity. "How would such a lout learn the language of the conquerors?"

"Be still, you fool," Ohlgren's metallic voice clicked in

German. "If he was there only two minutes before the dog barked he must have heard our toast to the Fuehrer! You think he would not recognize that name? Bah! I thought I told you to double the guard while they are on the island!"

"But, sir," the steward faltered, "we—we have caught him —and if there are others they will not leave here alive—"

"Silence!" Ohlgren's voice rose still higher and he flourished a massive fist. "You think we want killing here? *Gott im Himmel!* There must be no trouble—no investigations. Up to now everything has gone well. But this! We must put the problem before the Captain at once!"

He turned and led the way through a pantry and a huge, dark dining-room. Beyond, Barney caught a glimpse of the lounge that occupied the entire front of the house. It was an immense room and luxurious beyond anything the boy had ever seen. Deep, soft chairs, upholstered in leather, clustered about little islands of light. There were thick rugs on the floor, and the walls were hung with mounted sailfish and tarpon.

On one of the lighted tables at the left there was a tray of glasses, siphons and bottles. And lolling in chairs beside it were two naval officers in immaculate dress whites. The younger of the pair sprang up in alarm when Ohlgren pushed

Barney forward. He was youthful and smooth-shaven, with a fresh, pink complexion. His laugh, when he saw he was facing only a mud-spattered boy, sounded relieved.

But it was the other officer who held Barney's eyes. He was over forty, solid and broad-shouldered. His skin was weathered like a seaman's. Below a close-clipped mustache his firm mouth and jaw looked as if they had been carved out of mahogany.

He spoke now, in a booming, quarter-deck bass. "Well, Herr Ohlgren, so we have a visitor, eh?"

Ohlgren was apologetic. "I'm terribly sorry, *Herr Kapitan*. Perhaps by accident this boy came ashore. My men are searching now to make sure he was alone."

"Have you questioned him?"

"Not yet. He's one of these ignorant Americans, of course, so we'll have to talk to him in English."

The Captain leaned forward, elbows on his knees, and fixed Barney with his stern, gray eyes.

"What's your name, my boy?" The English words, spoken easily and with only the slightest accent, caught Barney by surprise. He hesitated, then stammered his answer.

The questions proceeded. Where did he live? How old was he? What was he doing on Caldee Island?

"I—lost my way in the dark," the boy replied in a low voice. "My boat grounded an' then I saw a light. Thought I could ask where I was an' get my bearings."

"He is lying," Kramer muttered in German. "Many times he has been here."

The Captain ignored the interruption. "And then the dog found you," he continued. "Where were you at that moment?"

Barney pointed at the nearby window. "Out there," he said.

"And did you hear our voices?"

The boy bent his head in assent. "I couldn't tell what anybody said, but I heard folks talking."

"Hmm!" The Captain rose and paced over to the window, where he pulled up the blind and looked out. Rain dripped on the shrubbery just beyond the screen. His face was still impassive when he returned.

"What do you propose to do about this, Ohlgren?"

"First of all we must take you and the *Herr Leutnant* back at once. There may be no time to lose. The ship will be waiting at the rendezvous?"

The Captain nodded. "She is to be there from darkness until we arrive. But what about the boy?"

"He has heard too much!" Kramer hissed. "There is only one thing to do with him."

Ohlgren turned on the speaker coldly. "You are to blame for that," he said. "And remember—there will be a search for him."

The steward bowed. "I have thought of that, Herr Ohlgren. His boat will be found by his friends, floating bottom up, somewhere at a distance from here. There will be nothing to show he has been near the island. We can trust the men for that."

Ohlgren considered. "Very well," he snapped. "Take him away and do what you have to do. We are leaving immediately. Tell Kurt to warm up the engines."

The Captain lifted his hand. "One moment," he rumbled. "I see nothing to be gained by a killing. True, he may have heard and seen too much. He cannot go back to his people. But there is room for him aboard my ship. He will be interned in Germany when we make port."

Barney, who had been standing stoically, trying to pretend that he understood none of the conversation, saw a gleam of hope in the black emptiness of his terror. He drew a long, unsteady breath. Kramer, close by his side, was too angry to notice. His face had gone white and hard and he seemed to be choking back the words he wanted to say.

After a tense second, the steward clicked his heels, bowed without speaking, and left the room.

The Captain smiled. "A good man, no doubt," he said, "but perhaps a little hasty. Come," he beckoned to the younger officer. "We must be ready to leave in a minute or two."

The servant, Fritz, hurried after them and came back a moment later with two small bags. Ohlgren towered over Barney, staring down at him impersonally. Then he spoke in English.

"It isn't often," he remarked, "that a democratic swine like you gets a reprieve. You are lucky to be young. Perhaps they'll make an honest Nazi out of you."

Barney didn't trust himself to answer. The reaction from being so close to death made his knees tremble, and there was a tight sensation in his throat. Then he heard light, quick footsteps behind him and turned his head in time to see Kramer returning. The steward had a coil of stout cord in his hand.

"These fishermen are sometimes good swimmers," he explained to Ohlgren. "Just as a precaution—"

And before Barney could move, his arms were pulled

together behind him. He felt the cord whip tightly around his wrists, and the knot was tied with a quick jerk that cut into his flesh.

The two officers reappeared, ready to take their leave. They wore long, dark slickers over their uniforms, and oilskin covers protected their natty white caps. There was no lingering for conversation. Fritz opened the front door and the party walked briskly down to the dock, with Barney and Kramer at their heels.

The engines of the *Valkyr* were purring smoothly and the three men of her crew stood stiffly at attention as the group stepped aboard. Ohlgren and his guests went from the cockpit into the roomy cabin, forward. "Bring the boy in," the owner called to Kramer in German. "He'll see less, inside, and he won't be tempted to jump overboard."

Barney blinked as the steward pushed him into the brightly lighted compartment. On a smaller scale it was almost as sumptuous as the Castle lounge. There were deep bunks along the sides, comfortable chairs, a table and a cabinet filled with glass and china. The whole interior was finished in gleaming teakwood and mahogany. Thick black velvet curtains covered the portholes, so that no light could escape.

At once the throb of the engines deepened and the deck tilted under the boy's feet. The cruiser was swinging out of the harbor, stealing along through the rain and the darkness. Where she was headed, or what would happen to him when she reached her destination, Barney could only guess.

## 6

"YOU can sit there, on the floor in the corner,"
Kramer told Barney.

The boat must be leaving the pass and bucking
the seas in the inlet, for she had begun to pitch and roll a
little. The boy slumped back against the after bulkhead and
closed his eyes. His mind had begun to work again, and he
figured that if he appeared completely exhausted they might
let him alone. Right now he had to think things out.

At least he was alive and he meant to stay alive. Tomorrow there would be plenty of excitement at home. Perhaps
Anna would break her promise and tell his father where he
had gone. The fishermen would load their shot-guns and
start for Caldee. Word would probably be sent to Slug
Martin, and the Army would investigate his disappearance.
He wished he could be around to see it all happen.

Bitterly he reproached himself for not telling his family what he was doing. John Cannon would have seen the rashness of his undertaking and found some other way to deal with Ohlgren's gang. As it was, there might be no proof that he had discovered treachery on Caldee. Kramer's plan was smart. The overturned boat, drifting somewhere miles away in the channel, would be the only clue to what had befallen him. The tide and the rain would obliterate any sign of his landing or any tracks he might have left in the marsh mud. "Death by drowning"—that's what the coroner would say.

And meanwhile where would he be? The German Captain had spoken once or twice of "his ship." That might mean almost anything—a submarine—a merchantman converted for raiding—a cruiser or destroyer. She must be lying offshore now, and not too far away, for the *Valkyr's* tanks would hardly hold enough fuel for a long voyage.

The big motorboat was picking up speed now. He could feel the thrust and drive of her powerful engines and hear the rush of water past her sides. She must be doing twenty knots or better.

After a few minutes Ohlgren and the Captain went up the little companionway to the glass-enclosed bridge. The Lieutenant poured himself a drink and sat back in his chair thumbing a copy of an American picture magazine. Some of the articles in it made him flush and frown, and once he laughed in scornful amusement.

"These fools!" he exclaimed. "They tell their readers the U-boat menace is under control—that convoys and airplane patrols have stopped us on the Atlantic Coast. That is fine news for the stupid Yankees, no? They will not work so hard now—take a holiday and think they have won the war! This is something for the Admiral to see."

He ripped the page out of the magazine, folded it and put it in his pocket. Then he looked over at Barney.

"You, boy," he said, in rather stiff English, "do your folk think such stuff is true?"

Barney gaped at him, his eyes blank. "What stuff?" he asked.

The Lieutenant colored. "You will address officers as 'sir,' " he snapped. "I asked if your folk believe such tales as are in this paper here—that the U-boats have been beaten off —that there will be no more sinkings."

"Why—no, sir." The boy hesitated. "We know there's plenty o' ships being sunk if that's what you mean. An' plenty o' subs, too."

The young officer scowled at him as if trying to decide

how that last remark should be taken. Finally he dismissed it with a shrug, lighted a cigarette and turned back to his reading.

The *Valkyr* had been traveling fast for half an hour when Ohlgren ordered the engines throttled down to quarter-speed. From the motion, Barney figured they were steering in a slow circle. Then the Captain called his junior officer to the foot of the companion.

"Try them on the oscillator," he ordered. "It's in that little door at the left."

The Lieutenant opened a small cupboard and Barney saw an instrument inside. It looked somewhat like a telegraph key. The young man took a pair of head-phones off a hook in the cupboard and slipped them on over his ears. Then he began to tap the key slowly. If he was using a code, Barney was sure it wasn't Morse. The clicking continued for ten or fifteen seconds and seemed to follow a regular pattern—"*tick . . . tick-tick . . . tick-tick.*" After that the Lieu-tenant stopped and listened.

"They heard me and answered," he called up the steps. "They're surfacing now—not more than five hundred meters away."

So "they" must be the crew of a submarine. Barney's heart

sank. He was going to be a prisoner on one of those hated undersea raiders.

The *Valkyr's* engines were thrown into neutral now and she lay rocking in the swells while the men on her bridge searched the black water around her with tense concentration.

Kramer stood up and pulled a neatly folded bandanna out of his coat pocket. "On your feet!" he ordered Barney sharply.

In an instant he had bound the handkerchief tightly over the boy's eyes. "It is just as well," he remarked, "if you do not see too much."

Barney heard the Captain's deep voice bellow across the water and then came a fainter answering hail. The boat's engines sent her churning slowly ahead. There was more shouting, and the *Valkyr* was maneuvered into position alongside another craft. He could hear the creak of cordage as mooring lines were pulled taut.

The Captain thanked Ohlgren as they came down the companion steps. "I trust," he added, "that you won't be placed in any difficulties by tonight's affair."

Ohlgren laughed. "There'll be some questions asked, of course. But why should we be suspected? The lad drowned, that's all."

Hands gripped both of Barney's arms and he was hustled out to the cockpit, then lifted to the narrow deck of the motorboat. The rain was still falling, for he felt the cold drops on his face and neck.

"Up with him," ordered the Lieutenant. The boy's arms and legs were seized by several men, and he was tossed upward to be caught by strong hands from above. When they set him on his feet he could feel wet steel deck plates under his bare soles. He was led along for several yards, till his shoulder bumped against some upright structure.

"Here," said a strange voice in German, "he can't climb down the ladder. His hands are tied. Get ready to catch him below, Grauner."

There was a sickening second when he felt himself falling through space. Then he landed with a jolt in a pair of mighty arms. The man who caught him seemed to be huge, stripped to the waist and slippery with sweat. He gave a deep grunt as he set Barney down. The blindfolded boy wondered what sort of giants they used to man these Nazi subs.

The compact space below decks seemed crowded with men and machinery. There was a close, oily smell in the heavy air, in spite of whirring ventilator fans. Barney was handed along from man to man, stumbling over obstructions, bumping into unseen bulkheads and stanchions. He was pushed through a narrow door into a second chamber, and there, at last, someone pulled the folded bandanna from his eyes.

The glare of electric bulbs dazzled him for a moment. Then he saw the blond young Lieutenant standing in front of him. The officer eyed him coldly. "As a prisoner, you will be confined to this compartment for the next twenty-four hours," he told him in stilted English. "Afterward, if your behavior is good, we may find something for you to do."

He swung on his heel toward a boyish-looking sailor who stood at attention. "You, Hans," he snapped in German, "untie his hands and put him in the bunk where Schmidt was. See that he gets food when the watch eats. Don't let him out of here until I send for him. *Heil Hitler!*"

The young sailor answered with a stiff-armed salute and a low-voiced "*Heil Hitler.*"

When the Lieutenant was gone, Barney looked about him. He was in a steel chamber, some thirty feet long by a dozen wide, and not more than six feet high. A triple tier of bunks ran along the sides—twenty-four of them in all. There were heavy steel doors at either end, and the bulkheads were covered with a confusing tangle of pipes, valves, gauges and other mechanical gadgets.

The young German was looking at him curiously. "You turn," he said in laborious English. "I make der rope off."

Barney turned obediently and the cord that bound him was pulled free. He rubbed his wrists gingerly. They were swollen and there were deep, purple channels in the flesh. His fingers were so numb he could barely bend them.

"Here," said Hans. "Dees bed iss for you. Der man Schmidt ve lost overboard—he had it before." He pointed to a bunk in the lower tier at the end of the row, and Barney sat down on its edge. The thin mattress was hard under him, and the blanket was of some rough material that didn't feel like wool or cotton.

"You lie down now," Hans nodded. "If you like, maybe you sleep."

Barney was glad to stretch out in the narrow berth. He was more tired than he had realized after his ordeal, and he felt chilly in the draft from the ventilators, for his clothes were still damp. He pulled the blanket up over him, closed his eyes, and turned on his side with his face toward the bulkhead.

He wasn't yet ready for sleep. Too many things had happened to him in the last three hours and he wanted to think some of them out. He knew that by now the *Valkyr* would be well on her way back to Caldee Island. Unless something unexpected happened, it would be midnight before his father and mother got really worried about him. And long before any action was taken, Ohlgren's men would have done a thorough job with his boat. He felt a pang of pity for his mother and Anna. They would take it hard, he knew. Then he thought of Slug Martin and grinned. That tough Texan might have a fair idea of what had happened, and he wouldn't swallow any tales of a drowning accident. There might be some fireworks before Slug got through!

He heard no sound of motors, and the slow rocking of the submarine told him she must still be lying on the surface. Most of the men were evidently on deck, for nobody entered the room. He imagined that submarine sailors would spend all the time they could in the open air, even on a rainy night.

Sometime later, when he had begun to drowse off, the muffled roar of the Diesels woke him. There were sharply shouted orders and the clang of steel hatches and doors being closed. Then he felt the structure in which he was imprisoned tilt slowly lengthwise. They were submerging!

Barney had a rough working knowledge of submarines from his talks with men in the Coast Guard and the Navy. He knew that the Diesel engines were used only on the surface, to run the ship and charge the batteries. As soon as an undersea craft submerged, the engines stopped and all power was supplied by the batteries. That was what bothered him now. The Diesels were still pounding away, although he could swear the submarine was smoothly descending.

He sat up in the bunk, bumping his head on the frame of the one above, and stared at Hans.

"Are we diving?" he asked.

The German boy grinned, pleased that he could understand. "Ya, so," he nodded. Then he glanced at a gauge on the bulkhead nearby. "Ten meters," he announced.

Barney calculated. He knew a meter was a little over a yard, so they must be more than thirty feet below the surface. Then he felt the submarine level off on an even keel. That would mean they were cruising at periscope depth. And still he heard the puzzling throb of the engines. He wondered if he could convey the question in his mind to his young guard.

"Look," he began, "don't you run on the batteries when you're under water?"

Hans wrinkled his brows in a valiant effort to make sense out of the words, but the task seemed to be beyond him. He shrugged his shoulders and smiled again good-naturedly.

At that moment Barney was tempted to ask his question in German. The words were on the tip of his tongue but common sense warned him in time. So far none of them suspected that he had any knowledge of their language. It was a secret that might come in handy some day if he could keep it.

He lay down again and shielded his eyes with one arm. After a minute or two, the door from the control room opened and a number of sailors came in. They were a hard-muscled, husky-looking lot in their sleeveless undershirts and breeches. Most of them were young—nineteen or twenty, Barney thought. But several were veteran seamen. They came and stood by his bunk, staring down at him as if he were some rare beast in a cage. Then part of the group went on into the next compartment and the rest prepared to turn in.

The last man to approach the bunk was Grauner, the giant sailor who had caught him when he was dropped down the conning-tower hatch. Barney knew him by his huge, blacksmith's arms and barrel chest. Peeping from under the shelter of his elbow, the boy could see a scarred and bloated face with thick, black brows meeting above a broken-bridged nose. The man gave him only a brief glance before swinging up to the top bunk in the tier, directly over Barney's. Then somebody turned a switch and the bright lamps went out leaving only a dim blue night-light.

The men were all in their bunks now and a few were already snoring. There was some scattered, low-voiced conversation and then quiet. Barney lay still, trying to get used to his strange surroundings. It was no use to spend time crying over spilt milk. His rash visit to Caldee was past and done. The best thing he could do now was adjust himself to being a prisoner aboard an enemy submarine. Maybe some opportunity for escape, still unforeseen, would present itself. He had to be ready for that one desperate chance.

Drowsily he considered the people he had to deal with. The Captain was a man of courage and brains. He had all the earmarks of a good sailor and an able commander. Saving Barney's life had been an act more of hard sense than of kindness, but the boy felt he would get fair treatment as far as the Captain was concerned.

The Lieutenant was of a different stripe. His youth made him less certain of himself, perhaps more proud and domineering. There was weakness in him somewhere, Barney thought.

Young Hans seemed a stupid, decent sort, not at all the type of vicious Hun that he had expected to find on a U-boat. But there was one at least in the crew who went even beyond those expectations. The face of the big man, Grauner, haunted Barney still. It was a brute face, cruel, brooding, scarcely human. Backed by the force of that gigantic body it was a terrible face.

The boy turned over and sighed. The next instant he had fallen into a heavy, troubled sleep.

# 7

ARNEY had no idea how long he had slept when
Hans shook him by the shoulder. He half remembered rousing once when the watch was changed
and the men piled out of their bunks. The bright lights were
on again now, and there was nobody in the steel-walled
room except the tow-haired German boy and himself.

"Somedings to eat," grinned Hans. He held a tin plate of
food and an enameled cup. Barney sat up and took the plate
in his hands. On it was a heap of what looked like pale hash,
an iron spoon and a chunk of hard black bread. The cup
contained lukewarm water.

It wasn't an appetizing meal, but Barney was hungry. He
tried a spoonful of the nameless food and found it tasted
better than he expected. There was some sort of meat in it,
and vegetables. He thought it must have been kept in dehy-

84

drated form, then soaked in water and warmed up. The bread was dry and practically tasteless.

"Don't you get white bread sometimes?" he asked his guard.

"Ya, somedimes," Hans replied. But because his vocabulary was too limited or because he was afraid of betraying a secret, he said no more.

Barney finished his breakfast, if breakfast it was, and gave the utensils back to the German youth.

"You like, huh?" Hans asked.

"Sure, it was all right. What time do you reckon it is?"

"Nine hours," grinned the other boy. "Iss goot vedder up dere, so ve stay under vater."

Barney stood up and walked back and forth in the narrow chamber to limber his muscles. His clothes had dried on him while he slept, and except for the soreness in his wrists, he felt as well as ever. Hans showed him the location of the tiny lavatory, built into the forward end of the compartment, and he washed his face and hands. To his surprise there was a bar of white soap there—a familiar American brand. He had heard the Jerries were short of soap. This must have been brought aboard from Caldee along with other supplies.

Restless, Barney paced up and down, looking at the mechanical gadgets along the bulkheads and trying to figure out their purpose. Hans made no objection to these investigations. He would probably have been willing to explain them if his English had been adequate to the task. But Barney didn't want to appear inquisitive so he asked no more questions. He found the depth gauge and read it. Forty-five meters. There was no sound of engines and no motion in the ship. They must be lying quietly on the bottom to avoid detection by scouting planes or blimps. He figured forty-five meters was nearly twenty-five fathoms—just about the depth of the outer bank, close to the coastwise shipping lanes.

The air was heavy and humid in the chamber, and there were beads of moisture on the gray-painted bulkhead plates.

After fifteen or twenty minutes the steel door from the control room was opened. Barney had a momentary glimpse of the mass of machinery crowding that vital center of the ship. Then the figure of the young Lieutenant blocked his view. The officer strode in and shut the door behind him.

"You may go out, Hans," he told the German boy. "There's work for you in the engine room."

When the sailor had departed, the Lieutenant sat on the edge of a bunk and indicated with a wave of the hand that

Barney should do the same. Then he crossed his legs in their neatly creased white ducks and lighted a cigarette.

"How do you like it?" he asked, blowing a puff of smoke upward.

"It isn't bad—sir," Barney answered quietly.

"So? You would like to stay here?"

"No, sir. It would drive me nuts, having nothing to do. I can work—"

"Quiet," the officer interrupted. "We will come to that later. For the present you may speak only when spoken to."

He leaned back, surveying the boy through insolent, half-closed eyes.

"You have been in Pennsylvania, not?" he asked, surprisingly.

Barney shook his head. "No, sir. Never further'n Norfolk, once."

"*Ach*, you provincial Americans," the young man laughed. "I have traveled more in your country than you." He chuckled once or twice as if remembering something.

"Six years ago," he said, "when I was of an age close to yours, some good, noble-hearted fools in New York had a plan. They thought it would make peace and understanding between our nations if we exchanged a few young boys and girls for one summer. So it was arranged. Fifty or sixty silly American children went on a ship to Germany, and the same number of Hitler youth came over to New York. I was one of those." He paused.

"We were well chosen. All of us with the right training and the proper party background. We were good at languages, intelligent and observant. We had our cameras and our orders.

"I think your government was asleep as usual. They paid very little attention to us. After a week of sight-seeing in New York, Philadelphia and Washington, we were taken to pleasant resorts in the mountains. Wealthy pacifist people took us into their families, one or two of us to each cottage. They expected us to become filled with their ideas of liberty and democracy—bah!"

He spat out the words as if they were bitter on his tongue. "Sometimes," he continued, "we were forced into arguments with American boys. They even sneered at our Fuehrer!" His voice trembled. "We were trained to hold our tempers, but it was hard. At the end of the summer we went back to the Fatherland with our pictures of docks and harbors and skyscrapers, and we had learned to speak your language and despise your softness."

Barney did not smile, but he looked at the Nazi's white hands and pink-skinned, almost girlish face and wondered about that word. Maybe softness, to this kind of man, meant just being kind and neighborly.

"Perhaps this bores you," the Lieutenant said sharply. "I see it conveys little to your dull, yokel mind. But remember, while you are on this ship, that we have had experience with you Americans. We know how to handle you. You will be a servant here, just as all democrats will be servants of the master race when we have won the war. Can you cook?"

The sudden question took Barney by surprise. "Why—not much," he stammered. "I can fry eggs an' beat up a mess o' flap-jacks—"

The officer held up an impatient hand. "That is unnecessary," he snapped. "A cook's helper is needed in the galley, to replace the stupid Schmidt who was drowned. So that you may not have time to become homesick, we will find other duties for you as well. I'll have you outfitted with decent clothes instead of those rags."

He rose, dropped his cigarette on the deck and trod on it. "Pick that up," he ordered, "and dispose of it. *Heil Hitler!*"

With that he clicked his heels, made a military half turn, and stalked out. When his stiff back vanished through the door, Barney grinned, picked up the flattened cigarette and threw it in the toilet. He thought he had not been wrong in his judgment of the submarine's junior officer.

Hans returned a moment later carrying a seaman's uniform, patched but clean. He held the clothes out to Barney, indicating that he should put them on. "You got job, eh?" he grinned.

"Yeah, I reckon so, but he didn't say when I'd start," said Barney. "What's the Lieutenant's name?"

"*Der Herr Leutnant? Leutnant Rasch.*"

"An' what do you call the Captain?"

"*Herr Kapitan Von Sturm.*" The lad's voice was reverent. "He iss very fine officer."

Barney nodded. "He looks like it. You been in the U-boats long?"

"Seven mont's," Hans grinned. "Four mont's since I make port."

"Gee! you fellows really stay out a while, don't you? Do you figure Lieutenant Rasch wants me to start in the galley right off?"

The German shook his head. "Not yet. He vill tell you."

Barney went back to his bunk and sat down to wait. Then he heard the door opening again and caught a scared look on Hans' face. The man who entered was the giant Grauner, crouching to clear the six-foot door frame.

"Go on back to the engine room, you," he rumbled at the German boy, and made a threatening pass at his head with a huge, bear-paw hand.

Hans scuttled out and the big man slouched on a bunk facing Barney. His thick lips twisted into something like a grin. "Hiya, punk," he said.

The words and the accent were pure American. Barney stared at him, speechless.

"Yeh," Grauner nodded. "I can talk your lingo pretty good. I lived in the States six-seven years. Maybe you like to hear somebody talk like that, huh?"

"It—it sort o' took me by surprise," Barney answered. "But it does sound good. A lot o' you people seem to know English."

"Oh, sure—out of school-books," the man shrugged. "But not me. I was the strong man in a circus, back home. Then the bad days come. What you call—inflation. Money was no good. I got out an' took a ship for America, an' right off they signed me up for a rassler. Boy, I made good dough, too! Maybe you heard o' me, only not by my real name. They called me the Purple Devil, an' I rassled all over—Boston,

New York, Philadelphia, Chicago, St. Louis—in all the big arenas.

"The guys I was meetin' was plenty tough, an' anything went. Eye-gougin'—strangle-holds—all the tricks I learnt. I used to wear a sort o' hood but it didn't save my face. My nose was busted more times'n I can count—my jaw once—an' plenty o' ribs. But what I done to the other guys was a shame!"

He rubbed a huge hand over his bristly jowl reminiscently, and there was a light of battle in his squinty eyes.

"Yeh," he sighed. "I was cleanin' up. Only one night I slammed a Russian acrost the ring-post an' broke his back. When he croaked I was in a jam, an' had to get out fast. So that's how I got to be gunner aboard a pig-boat."

He stood up as straight as the deck above would allow and stretched his immense arms. "It's like old times to gab with an American once in a while," he said. "Even a half-growed punk like you. I'll be seein' ya." And with that he shambled out again.

Barney gave a silent whistle and mopped his damp forehead with his sleeve. This was a different Grauner from the one who had troubled his dreams. He seemed less dangerous, though just as formidable.

When Hans came back it was with a message. Barney was to report to the galley at once. The German boy led the way through the control room and along a narrow passageway, and opened the door of a tiny room that seemed full of shiny cooking equipment. What really crowded the place was the cook himself. He was a pasty-faced, crop-headed man with a bulging stomach. He wiped his fat hands on a dirty apron and glared at Barney.

"So!" he jabbered in German. "They expect me to make use of this dirty American! He will no doubt poison all the food. What does he know how to do?"

Hans translated the question and Barney replied that he could cook a little and wash dishes. This didn't appear to satisfy the cook, who grunted and threw up his hands in a hopeless gesture.

"Here!" he said, putting a big paring-knife in Barney's hand and pointing to a pan of potatoes in the corner behind him.

The boy squeezed past and started to work peeling them. Once in a while the fat man darted a suspicious look at him and muttered under his breath. When Barney finished that task he was given others, equally unexciting.

The cook knew only a few dozen words of English and

most of those were swear words. But by making vigorous signs with his pudgy fingers he managed to convey his orders.

When the noon meal was ready, Barney carried a steaming kettle of stew to the forward and after bunk rooms, where the men ladled out their helpings into tin plates. This course was accompanied by black bread and followed by a kind of steamed pudding with raisins in it, then mugs of coffee. Much to Barney's surprise it was real coffee, strong and sweet. He asked Hans about that later and learned that the U-boat had picked up several sacks of South American coffee and sugar while she was raiding in the Caribbean.

When the utensils had been washed, Lieutenant Rasch sent for Barney and turned him over to the bosun, a chunky, black-haired sailor from the Hamburg docks. His name was Blohm and his English was no better than the cook's. However, there was no mistaking what he meant when he handed the boy a rag and a can of polish and pointed to the brightwork in the control room. For the next two hours Barney labored hard, rubbing the metal till he could see his face in its gleaming surface. While he worked he tried to figure out what the dozens of different handles and levers and valves were for. Some of them had German words embossed on them but they told him little.

While the submarine lay on the bottom, the control room was a quiet place. One sailor remained there, leaning against the bulkhead and watching Barney work without much interest. Every fifteen minutes the man went to various gauges, took their readings, and jotted them down in a small notebook.

Finally the bosun came through and looked over the shiny brightwork critically. He nodded, showed the boy where to put the rag and polish, and indicated gruffly that he was free to go back to his quarters.

By this time Barney was gaining a fair idea of how the space inside the ship was arranged. He had had a glimpse of the forward torpedo room which filled the tapering, cone-shaped bow. The compartment where he had his bunk was next. Then came the control room, and next aft were the captain's cabin and the commissioned officers' cubicles, opening off a passage two feet wide. Beyond the galley was another bunk room, smaller than the forward one; then, through another passage, the engine room, where there was just room to squeeze between the long banks of cylinders on the two big Diesels; and last of all came the after torpedo room.

He judged that the submarine must be close to three hundred feet long, over all—probably around eight hundred tons. Her crew, including officers and men, would number nearly fifty.

When he returned to the bunk room he found most of the berths occupied. The men did little talking. Many of them rested or slept, but two or three were reading paper-covered books. He saw one bearded veteran industriously knitting a sock. They still showed enough curiosity in the new passenger to stare at him as he passed, but nobody spoke to him. He lay down and shut his eyes, trying to sleep.

A few minutes later an electric bell shrilled and a voice came with metallic resonance through a loudspeaker. "Stand by for surfacing."

A dozen of the men—members of the watch on duty—sprang out of their berths and ran to their stations in various parts of the ship. The engines began to throb. Then there was a long hiss of compressed air as seawater was forced out of the ballast tanks. The deck took an upward tilt.

Hans looked across at the American and grinned. "Maybe you hear some shooting," he said. "Dey pick up sound of ship coming."

# 8

THE submarine rose rapidly, and Barney watched the needle on the depth gauge move from 40 meters to 30, finally to 10. There the craft leveled off, cruising at periscope depth. The door stood open and he could see what went on in the control room, now crowded with men.

In the center of the room rose the two thick pillars of the periscopes. At one of them Captain Von Sturm stood, his broad shoulders bent, his hands on the grips that turned the periscope and his face close to the eyepiece.

He adjusted the device once more, then stood tense and motionless for perhaps five seconds. Barney saw him lift his hand and give a quiet order which he could not hear. A seaman turned the valves of the hydraulic mechanism that lowered the periscope, and at once the throbbing tempo of the engines quickened. A quartermaster, at the small wheel in front of the gyrocompass, repeated the course the Captain gave him and spun the wheel to starboard. Barney could feel the craft swerve obediently. In another moment they were charging along under water at a speed that must have been better than ten knots.

Grauner came through the door into the crew's quarters and took a blouse and a sweater out of his sea-bag. He pulled them on over his naked torso and winked at Barney as he went by. "Job for a gunner up there pretty quick," he said.

In three or four minutes the U-boat's speed was reduced and the Captain ordered the periscope raised again. A quick look seemed to satisfy him. "Surface!" he ordered. "Take battle stations!"

Barney saw the depth gauge needle move toward zero, and heard the rush of waves as the superstructure broke water. Then the conning-tower hatch must have been opened for he caught a whiff of cool, salty air. Men were swarming quickly up the ladder. Nobody seemed to be paying much attention to the boy at that moment and he was strongly tempted to follow the group on deck.

He crossed to the foot of the companion and had placed one hand on the rungs when he felt a strong grip on his shoulder. Blohm, the bosun, stood beside him.

"*Nein,*" the man growled, shaking his head. "*Verboten.*"
Firmly he led Barney back into the bunk room and closed
the steel door, leaving him alone in the compartment.

He was nervous and excited. Two or three times he paced
the length of the narrow deck space between the berths.
Then, just as he was turning, there was a jarring crash overhead. He sat down on the edge of his bunk, gripping it with
tense fingers, wondering what had happened. Again the hull
shook to a heavy report and it was followed in a few seconds
by a faint sound of cheering. He knew then that what he
had heard was the firing of the big deck gun just above him.
They must have hit their target, whatever it was. He shivered a little.

There was no more shooting. Instead he heard shouts in
the control room and the loud clang of a closing hatch. An
instant later the submarine began moving rapidly forward.
The deck canted at a steep angle, and as the door opened
men stumbled in, clutching at the bunk rails for support.
One of them was the huge ex-wrestler, his scarred face looking as black as a thundercloud.

He ripped off his sweater and flung it down with an angry
gesture.

"I'd have sunk the swine with another shot!" he grumbled in German to the man nearest him. "One more chance was all I wanted! But would they give it to me? No!"

"We didn't get down any too quick," the other sailor answered. "If they saw us there'll be—"

There was a deafening roar and the submarine lurched as if she had been struck by a giant fist. Barney was flung hard against the bulkhead at the back of the berth.

"Depth charge!" The cry rang harshly in the steel chamber, and there was a sound of panic in the echoing words. Lifting himself to a sitting position, Barney saw men strewn along the alley, struggling to get up. The slope of the deck had become even steeper. He wondered how soon the water would come rushing in to drown them all like trapped rats.

But to his amazement the sailors had regained their composure. One of them laughed as he clambered into his berth. "Not as close as I thought at first," he told the man in the bunk below. "And look at the way the *Herr Kapitan* is taking her down! At a hundred and eighty meters those things won't even shake us!"

Barney did some multiplication in his head. A hundred and eighty meters was close to six hundred feet. These new U-boats must be built more solidly than any undersea craft he had ever heard of, if they could stand such pressures.

Five minutes later he felt the submarine level off, and saw by the depth gauge that the seaman's guess had not been far off. The engines had stopped and they were resting somewhere on the bottom, a hundred fathoms below the surface.

The bosun came through and called a number of names. Picked crewmen were sent forward and aft to check on possible damage to the hull. They reported on their return that they had found nothing amiss. But as the hours dragged by there was a feeling of tension in the cramped quarters. The officers knew it and ordered a round of beer served out. Barney was put to work carrying the foaming metal cups to the bunk rooms.

The men lay relaxed, trying to avoid exertion in the heavy air. Some of them played listless games of cards, read, quarreled or slept. When the boy returned to his berth he found Grauner squatting on the edge of it.

"Sit down," said the big gunner. "I ain't tryin' to crowd you out—just keepin' low where it's easier to breathe."

"What happened on deck?" Barney asked. "Was that a depth charge from a destroyer?"

"Naw!" The giant still sounded disgusted. "There was an old freighter goin' along—all by herself. I missed the first shot, but the second got her forward, right under the bridge. We was loadin' again when one o' them fast two-engine bombers come over. We could have drilled him with our antiaircraft gun, but no—the Cap'n ordered a crash dive. All the plane had was a little bomb an' it was just dumb luck it landed so close. But while they keep cruisin' around overhead, we don't dare surface."

Two sailors arguing in the next tier of bunks turned to Grauner. "Hey, Big One, you speak the boy's filthy language," one of them called. "Ask him if it is true that the American government shoots people if they are caught driving automobiles."

Grauner turned the query into his own kind of English and Barney answered with an emphatic "No."

That didn't satisfy the disputants. One of them had heard it for a fact, he insisted. The U-boats had sunk so many tankers that no more gasoline was reaching the coast ports.

"Well," Barney told Grauner, "gas is short, but there's a right smart amount of it being sold. Folks don't get as much as they used to, but they still drive their cars, an' nobody shoots 'em."

The huge gunner's translation into German was fairly accurate. The two men nodded and chuckled. "We'll make them yell for help—no doubt of that! They're beginning to feel the pinch!"

Another sailor joined the conversation. "If they were half as clever as our German chemists, going without oil wouldn't bother them. I told you the Yankees were stupid, Heinrich."

"Shut up, Fritz, you big-mouth!" one of the first pair warned in a low voice.

"All right," the man called Fritz muttered. "But why worry? The young fool doesn't know a word of German."

Barney tried to look as blank as possible. He wondered what Fritz had been talking about. Apparently he had been on the verge of telling some kind of secret. "German chemists . . . going without oil wouldn't bother them . . ."

Those words seemed to be the key to an idea, but no sooner had it crossed Barney's mind than he discarded it. Running Diesel engines without oil was too fantastic. And yet—he thought of the steady throb of those Diesels while the U-boat was running submerged.

"How long you reckon we'll be staying down?" he asked Grauner with a pretended yawn.

"Till dark. Maybe four hours more. You ain't gettin' the heebie-jeebies, are you, punk? Got to learn to take it, in a pig-boat."

Barney lay back in the bunk and shut his eyes. He found he was breathing deeper in an effort to get enough air. Beads of moisture stood on the steel-work, and the men were sweating. After a while there was a hissing sound as someone in the control room opened the valve of an oxygen tank. Almost at once the breathing grew easier. The slight headache Barney had felt left him magically, and energy flowed back into his limbs.

Grauner gave his back a friendly pat that nearly knocked the wind out of him and stood up, stretching his powerful arms. Barney rolled over in the berth. In a moment he was asleep.

The next thing he knew somebody was shaking his shoulder. It was time to help the cook with the supper. He staggered back to the galley and for the next two or three hours he was too busy to think about the passage of time. Just as he was finishing the last of the dishes, the loudspeaker began to blare orders. The engines rumbled into action and the submarine moved upward on a long, easy slant.

It was a good twenty minutes before they surfaced. The Captain had searched the dark, surrounding sea through the periscope and found nothing. Only when he was satisfied that no fighting ships were lurking about the place did he order the forward hydroplanes up. The superstructure slid smoothly out of the sea, water draining from the midships vents with a gurgling roar. In another moment the conning-tower hatch was thrown open, and the clean air of the night came down through the ventilators.

"All right, men," Lieutenant Rasch ordered. "Take a turn on deck. Fifteen men at a time. No smoking."

The first group was above for half an hour. Barney, wondering if he would ever be allowed the same freedom as the crew, was taken by surprise when the bosun counted off the second batch and included him among them. He crowded with the others to the foot of the ladder and waited while the first lot descended.

In a moment he was climbing through the narrow opening, stepping out on the wet, heavy plates of the U-boat's deck. It was a starless, overcast night with a faint stir of air and a quiet sea. He stood close to the conning tower for a minute or two while his eyes became adjusted to the dark. Then, like the rest of the men, he began walking forward and aft inside the thin cables that served as hand-rails. It was good to stretch his muscles and pull deep draughts of fresh air into his lungs.

At its widest part, near the conning tower, the deck was

perhaps fifteen feet wide. It allowed a passage of three or four feet on each side of the steel-armored tower. A dozen paces forward a wicked-looking five-inch gun was mounted, and the same distance toward the stern there was a small anti-aircraft gun. Otherwise the deck was clear, except for the radio masts. Ammunition hatches and a collapsible windlass in the bows were sunk flush with the plates.

The men strolled restlessly or stood by the rail, talking in low voices. A few of them grumbled because they were not allowed to light cigarettes. Up by the deck gun Barney came upon Grauner. The one-time wrestler's teeth flashed as his thick lips parted in a grin. He patted the breech of the gun.

"This is my baby," he growled. "Sometime I'll show you what she'll do. Cute little piece, ain't she? Ever hear o' the destroyer *Halberson?* Lost with all hands—only I bet the papers ain't printed the news.Well, kid, it wasn't no torpedo got her. It was me an' my gun. Laid a shell right in her stern where she carried her depth charges, at a range o' four kilometers. Boom! Nothin' left but a grease spot on the ocean!"

Barney stared at the big man. "How come you to tangle with a destroyer on the surface?" he asked. "I thought no sub would dare try it."

"Not often—no," Grauner grinned. "This time I'm tellin'

you about was different. She was flankin' a convoy, see? We was surfaced but they didn't see us through the fog. But after they'd got past, the fog lifted. I was sightin' the gun, hopin' it would happen, an' soon as I got a fair look I let her have it. Those fellers on the destroyer—I bet they never knew what hit 'em!"

He took Barney's wrist and laid his hand on the steel block that formed part of the gun's breech. "Feel there," he said. "Little notches filed in the edge. Every one means a ship. Count 'em."

Barney counted under his breath. "Eleven—twelve—thirteen—fourteen! You mean you sunk all those yourself?"

"Ya, sure. All in this boat, too—in three trips out."

"Gosh! How many did they get with torpedoes?"

"Oh, maybe a dozen more. Torpedoes cost a lot o' money, an' only one out o' three or four hits what it's aimed at. A smart skipper with a ship that handles fast can dodge a tin fish by zigzaggin'. It's better to shell 'em any time we can work on the surface. They make it tough now, though. Everything's runnin' in convoys along this coast. The gunners have it easier down in the Gulf o' Mexico."

Grauner seemed to be in a talkative mood and Barney decided to risk another question. "How many U-boats do you reckon there are in these waters—say from Florida to New York?" he asked.

"Fifteen—twenty—I don't know," the gunner replied carelessly. "There was four squadrons come out together. Five or six boats in a squadron. Some get sunk. Some have engine trouble or can't get supplies an' have to go back. Some get orders to cruise in another place, like off Brazil or up on the northern convoy route. We been here by ourselves for a couple o' weeks—just us an' a Hornet squadron boat."

"Hornet squadron?" Barney asked quickly.

"That's what they call the three-hundred-an'-five to three-hundred-an'-forty-five class. They got a black an' yeller hornet painted on their conning towers."

"Do you see the other boat often?"

"Sometimes we come alongside at night an' swap cigarettes. Not lately—but she's around here someplace."

A whistle blew and the men started toward the hatch. Their turn on deck was over. Barney's eyes had become accustomed to the darkness. There was a break in the clouds overhead, and a few stars shone down. As the boy came abreast of the tower he looked up and saw the submarine's number painted there in huge white characters—U-432. Below the figures there was something else that he could barely make out in the faint starlight. It was a picture of a pale, coiled serpent, its head lifted as if about to strike. The body just behind the head widened out like a hood, and on it was painted a black swastika.

At the hatch entrance Barney found himself by Grauner's side.

"Say," he whispered. "What's the name o' this boat's squadron?"

"Name? Oh, sure—I get you. We're the Cobras—some sort o' poison snakes like they have in Asia."

9

THE U-432 was still on the surface when Barney turned in. But she must have submerged during the hours while he was asleep, for it was the call to surfacing stations, blaring harshly over the loud-speaker system, that woke him.

He tumbled out with the others and stood by, watching the rising indicator. The submarine lifted to periscope depth, then leveled off. In the control room, Lieutenant Rasch was twisting the handles of one of the periscopes. Through the open door Barney could see his face tense and pale with excitement. The young officer lifted one hand warningly and gave a course and bearing to the bosun. Then he ordered the periscope down and the U-boat gathered speed.

"Man the forward tubes," snapped Rasch. "Hold her on the new course for two minutes. I must go now and call the *Herr Kapitan*."

"Hmmh!" Grauner muttered. "Man the tubes, eh? Means a convoy, or somethin' too big for the gun."

Four men went through the door in the forward bulkhead and Barney caught a glimpse of the torpedo room. He was staring at the grim, circular openings of the torpedo chambers when the bosun hurried in from the control room.

"Come on," he shouted, "get these deck plates up! We'll need some spare fish."

Several men stooped to turn hand screws under the edges of the bunks and a moment later they lifted two sections of steel plates that had formed the floor of the passage between the berths. Barney scrambled into his bunk to get out of the way. Looking down he had expected to see storage batteries, for he knew they would occupy that space in an American submarine. Instead he saw the glistening, round sides of well-greased torpedoes! They were lying in racks, three deep, with just enough space between them for a man's body.

Blohm sprang down into the dark alley, and a little electric crane on an overhead track rumbled into position above him. Chains rattled down and the bosun made them fast to one of the long, deadly cylinders. As soon as he clambered out the torpedo was hoisted waist-high. A moment later it was gliding forward into the torpedo room.

The operation was repeated and then the deck plates clattered down once more. The torpedoes were standard size, 21 inches in diameter and nearly twenty feet long. Except for minor differences in the screw-propellers at the tail, they looked very much like those Barney had seen loaded aboard destroyers at Norfolk. He knew what was inside them, too. The head was filled with TNT—five or six hundred pounds of it. Then came a heavy-walled chamber holding enough compressed air to drive the powerful motor which filled the after part. There were control vanes or rudders on the tail, and last of all were the four-bladed twin propellers, one behind the other.

The U-boat was no longer speeding through the water. The Diesels were turning over slowly and Captain Von Sturm had replaced Rasch at the periscope. From the control room came his deep voice ordering the helmsman as he maneuvered into position. Then the loudspeaker barked a warning—"Ready forward tubes!"

There was a breathless wait before the order came. "Fire one!"

Compressed air hissed and the ship took the jolt of the recoil as the first torpedo was launched. Almost at once

Barney heard "Fire two!" And a few seconds later the order came for a crash dive.

Bulkhead doors were slammed shut, men ran to their stations and the submarine plunged steeply. There were five others besides Barney in the bunk room. He could see their faces, white and tense under the glare of the electric light. They were waiting, bracing themselves. Young Hans was praying with scared, soundless lips.

When it came it was less terrifying than the first depth charge attack Barney had been through. The U-boat lurched and groaned under the force of the explosion and the lights went out, but the boy was able to stay in his berth.

The ship was still diving. Three or four more distant blasts rocked the hull and then Blohm came in with a flashlight. "There's some damage aft," he growled. "Four of you go to the engine room and stand by to look for it. You, Froelich, help me check on this wiring."

"What was it—a convoy?" the man called Froelich asked.

"Huh? Come—get to work! Yes, it was a convoy. Tankers, but too well guarded. We were lucky to get down before a destroyer cut us in two."

"How much damage did the depth charge do?" Froelich asked.

"Nothing bad. There's a leak where some plates buckled. Shouldn't take long to make repairs. But"—he hesitated, flashed the light toward Barney, and dropped his voice—"don't tell anybody, but the Captain got hurt."

"What! the *Herr Kapitan?*"

"Yes—knocked down by the explosion and hit his head. He's unconscious. Shut up, now, and let's get these wires fixed."

Half an hour later the lights came on and Barney saw that the depth gauge registered less than fifty meters. The engines were still throbbing and the submarine was moving steadily forward. Then he was sent to the galley to help prepare a meal. It was several hours before he returned to the crew's quarters and most of the men were already in their bunks.

Grauner stood in the middle passage, filling the space, his huge arms resting on the two top berths. "So," he was saying, "we're headed south again. Bananas, boys! And knocking off those Gulf freighters with the gun is like shooting fish in a barrel!"

"*Donnerwetter!*" someone grumbled behind him. "South, eh? Why don't they order us back to St. Nazaire? Or, better—Wilhelmshaven? What I want is some decent German food and some nice German girls!"

"You can trust the Captain to have good reasons," another man answered mildly.

"The Captain? That's how much you know!" It was Froelich's voice, low and cautious. As Barney slipped past to his own bunk, he saw the other men turn on the speaker with questioning faces.

"What's this?" the big gunner growled.

"Well—maybe I shouldn't have spoken. I thought the rest of you had heard the news. Captain Von Sturm was knocked out by the depth charge and the *Herr Leutnant* is running the ship."

"What? Rasch? That young fool? Why, he's no sailor—"

Their comments were silenced by the opening of the after door. Blohm, the bosun, stood there scowling. "Less talk!" he snapped. "All hands to stations for surfacing. The announcer system's out of order so you'll have to pass along the commands. Get moving!"

Grauner pulled a sweater on over his head, and Barney could hear him muttering, "So—surfacing! In broad daylight with a destroyer looking for us! *Himmel*, what an officer!"

The submarine went up to periscope depth and Rasch had a look around before he surfaced. What he saw apparently satisfied him. "A fine fog!" he exclaimed, rubbing his hands.

"No planes will be out, and we can make time running on the surface. Just keep her on course, quartermaster."

Barney could see swirling eddies of mist through the conning-tower hatch as the deck crew went up the ladder. The control room was empty except for the steersman and a man wearing head-phones, listening for propeller sounds.

The boy went back into the bunk room but there was nothing to do there, and he would not be needed in the galley for another hour at least. He wasn't used to sitting still. Perhaps he could use the time profitably after all.

He yawned, got up and went casually forward to the "head." When he came out of the little cubicle none of the half dozen men in the quarters glanced at him. They had become so used to having a prisoner aboard that they no longer paid any attention to his movements. He strolled aft, went quietly through the control room as if he were on an errand, and entered the passageway.

Just as he reached the Captain's door, it opened. He saw the worried face of the pharmacist's mate and squeezed aside to let him pass. Then, as the door closed, he caught a muffled sound of groaning and jumbled, half-intelligible words. The Captain was delirious.

The pharmacist's mate had hurried to the control room.

Barney kept on in the opposite direction. The cook was asleep in the galley, snoring loudly, and the few men in the after bunk room hardly looked up as the boy passed. Shutting the door behind him he found himself in the narrow, ten-foot passage that led back to the engine room. It was lighted by one small bulb overhead. Beyond the next bulkhead he could hear the rumble of the Diesels and the voices of the engine crew. But here in the passageway he was completely alone for the moment.

Right beside him there was a tight-fitting door. His hand went out to the latch, sunk flush with the steel panel. This was what he had come for—to discover what lay behind the bulkheads of the passage. It was the one part of the ship he had not been able to fit into the deck-plan he had charted in his mind.

Barney listened a moment but heard no approaching footsteps. He turned the handle softly. The door wasn't locked as he had feared. It opened outward, and he looked into a dark cavern filled with the dull gleam of metal. There was an immense tank of some sort, and above it coils of stainless steel tubing. From the pipes came a low, continuous, swishing sound.

For a long moment the boy stared, trying to make sense

out of what he saw. Then, silently, he pushed the panel shut. He had just turned and was taking a step in the direction of the engine room when the door in front of him opened. The man who came through was stripped to the waist and glistening with sweat. He recognized him as one of the Diesel mechanics.

Barney's stride faltered but the man gave him only a careless glance as he shoved past. As the forward door clanged shut the youngster drew a deep, shaky breath. He had a feeling that luck was with him. If the mechanic had caught him peeping into that hidden mass of tanks and tubes he would certainly have been in trouble. Even if he had been moving forward instead of aft, his presence in the passage would have looked fishy.

With greater boldness he stepped to the engine room door and opened it. The engineer officer looked around as he entered. His eyebrows lifted questioningly. "Who sent you and what do you want?" he asked in German, raising his voice above the roar.

Barney shrugged his shoulders and made no answer. Then his eye fell on a heap of rags in a sheet-iron box by his foot. He reached down and picked one up, holding it out to the engineer as if to ask what he wanted done.

The man grinned. "All right—goot!" he shouted in English with a heavy accent. "I show you, so."

He pointed to a long steel pipe which ran along the top of one row of cylinders, and made a rubbing motion with his hand. The metal looked spotless, but Barney went to work on it with a will. He had a special interest in those engines and here was his first opportunity to observe them closely.

It was hot there—more than a hundred degrees, he guessed—and hotter still just above the thundering, throbbing Diesels. As he rubbed and polished, his eyes were busy studying the huge machines. Familiar with two or three makes of American engines, he knew wide variations in design were to be expected. Even so, it was difficult to figure out how these big German plants worked.

One thing he looked for was the fuel injection system—the pump and nozzle that shot a charge of oil mist into the hot compression chamber to produce each power stroke. At first he saw nothing that even remotely resembled the usual fuel feed. He had finished the first bank of cylinders and was half-way down the room before he began to get the idea.

There was a short tube of heavy steel connecting each cylinder head with the pipe he was wiping. And he could see a corresponding set of tubes coming from another pipe on the farther side of the bank. If fuel oil passed through those inlets, where were the pumps to force it in under the necessary pressure?

Then he remembered the remark he had overheard in the bunk room. Something about getting along without oil. It still seemed a crazy idea, and yet—he had definite proof that the engines kept on running while the U-boat was submerged. That was strange enough in itself. It meant the Germans had found a way to get rid of poisonous exhaust fumes, and to operate without the big supply of air usually necessary to a Diesel motor. Was it possible that to accomplish those things they had developed a new kind of fuel?

Barney was so much occupied with his idea that he forgot to polish the pipe and stood gaping vaguely at the engines. The engineer stopped at his elbow and scowled. "What iss wrong?" he asked gruffly.

"N-nothing," the boy answered, startled. "Just hot and tired, I guess."

Hastily he began rubbing at the pipe again, and kept at it till he finished the job. Then he dropped the rag in the box and started forward. "It's time for me to help the cook," he explained. "I got to go to the galley now."

The officer nodded. "You do all right," he said. "I tell Blohm to send you here again ven you are not busy. *Heil Hitler!*"

Barney saluted awkwardly without answering. As he moved toward the door his eyes were following the two pipes through a maze of bends and valves till they passed through the bulkhead, along with another pair from the opposite bank of engines. If his guess was correct, whatever burned in those Diesels had its source in the tanks and tubing he had seen on the starboard side of the passage. Now, as he moved along the narrow aisle, he saw a similar door in the port bulkhead. Curiosity overcame his caution. Impulsively he reached for the handle and turned it, but this door was solidly locked.

Hardly had he drawn his hand away when a clatter came from the forward end of the passage and the same mechanic he had encountered earlier hurried through the open door. This time the man stared at him, obviously suspicious, as he brushed past.

Breathing quickly, he left the passageway and went on through the crew's quarters to the galley. The fat cook's nap was over. He gave the boy a surly scowl, thrust a big spoon into his hand and told him to stir the kettle of stew. Barney knew his explorations were over for that day. But he resolved, as he bent above the steaming pot, that he would find out more about the *Sea Snake's* fuel supply before he had been aboard much longer.

# 10

THEY moved steadily on the southward course, running submerged by day and surfacing at night for greater speed. No vessels were sighted for two days, and the submarine seemed to have more urgent business than lying in wait along the steamer lanes.

Barney was kept at work on a variety of tasks. He could not be sure whether Blohm suspected the trick by which he had gotten into the engine room or even knew he had been there. But it was certain that the bosun kept an extra sharp eye on him and gave him little leisure.

Twice he was allowed on deck for a few minutes at night. The air was warm on the surface, for the U-boat was in the midst of the Gulf Stream. Fish, big and little, cut patterns of glowing phosphorescent light around the slim hull, and the wake stretched brightly astern. Sometimes Barney wished the planes of the shore patrol would fly over in the dark and spot that shining line of foam. Then he thought of what would be likely to happen to him and hastily took back his wish.

Most of the food they had taken aboard from the *Valkyr* was gone now and the crew's rations were cut. They grumbled when Barney served out their meals in the bunk rooms. It was tasteless, unappetizing stuff and it never seemed to fill a man up. After helping to cook it, the boy could hardly bring himself to eat a mouthful, but hunger and the wish to keep alive made him clean his plate.

The packages and cans from which the food came were rarely marked except by numbers. Barney could only guess at what they contained, but he was fairly sure of some of the items. There were dehydrated cabbages, turnips and potatoes, which swelled to five or six times their dry bulk when cooked with water. And there was some kind of ground, dried meat that might be almost anything. The cook called it "pork," but Grauner and others in the crew insisted it was dog.

Once a day they were given a dessert of dehydrated apples or peaches. The bread was baked in the electric oven from a coarse gray-brown flour. It tasted like sawdust and Barney was positive that some of it was made from wood. The only parts of their diet that seemed to be present in unlimited quantities were water and vitamin tablets. Every man aboard was given three pills a day to make up for the vitamins lacking in the rest of the ration. As a consequence there were practically no cases of illness or signs of undernourishment.

Why fresh water should be so abundant was a question that bothered Barney at first. He got no satisfaction when he asked the cook about it, but Grauner was more talkative.

"It's them big evaporators, aft," he said. "We gotta have 'em anyway, because the engines use so much water in this special class o' new boats. What's piped through the ship an' used for drinkin' and bathin' ain't but a little part of it."

Barney packed that information away in his mind. It made another piece in the jigsaw puzzle he was trying to fit together. Evaporators—that's what he had poked his nose into when he opened the door off the passageway. No wonder the apparatus had somehow reminded him of a whisky still he had once seen in the woods on the mainland!

But why should the Diesel engines need an exceptionally large fresh water supply? Not for cooling, surely, because ordinary sea water was considered good enough in all the Diesels he knew. One part of the puzzle was still missing, and until he found it he was as much in the dark as ever.

Lieutenant Rasch worked the men hard on that southward voyage. Even though the stout pressure hull of the submarine had withstood the hammering of the depth charges, a considerable amount of damage had been done to air and water pipes and electric wiring. Each day the crew was divided into small squads and assigned to various repair jobs.

In off hours Barney was ordered to help one gang or another, and at mealtimes he had to carry food to the seamen, wherever they might be working. As a consequence he had a chance to visit parts of the vessel he had never seen before—the air-compressor room, next to the engines, and the after torpedo compartment. He kept his eyes and ears open but there was nothing in these places that brought him any nearer a solution of the fuel mystery.

From scraps of low-voiced talk he found out why the U-432 was traveling south. The Captain, it appeared, was badly hurt. Some said he had never regained consciousness after that blow on the head. They were taking him to some place where he could have the care of a surgeon.

There were black looks on the faces of some of the crew, and they took Rasch's loud commands in stony silence. Barney learned the reason at the end of the second day's cruising. He was in his bunk with his eyes closed when he heard whispering a few feet away.

"What about the Captain?" Grauner was asking. "Has he spoken today?"

The voice that answered was that of the seaman, Froelich. "Not a word. Nobody is allowed to see him but that stupid pharmacist's mate—and Rasch, of course."

"It's queer, that's what it is—a strong fellow like the *Herr Kapitan!* Did you see him fall?"

"Yes." Froelich's whisper was barely audible. "It was something he should have shaken off in ten minutes. A knock on the head that stunned him, that's all. But now—who knows what happened when the Lieutenant had him alone in his cabin?"

Grauner muttered an oath under his breath. It sounded like "*verdammte Nazi Schwein!*" But Barney couldn't be sure, and after that both men were silent.

The boy lay thinking for a long time. He had known that all the sailors aboard respected Von Sturm. Some of them, like the Captain, were veteran submariners, and a few had even served in the undersea boats in the first World War. One thing he remembered noticing was the absence of "heiling" among the crew. Rasch gave the Fuehrer's salute on all occasions and so did others of the younger commissioned officers. But more than once when a seaman had entered the bunk room with a *"Heil Hitler"* he had been answered only by a grunt or two and stolid silence.

Now the boy began to wonder. There seemed to be an under-current of discord running through the ship. Were the regular navy men loyal to the Nazi party? He suspected that some of them at least hated the Lieutenant who had taken over command. And if he had heard Grauner's exclamation aright there was something more going on—a political unrest that might be full of dynamite.

Barney went about his tasks with apprehension the next day. He had come to expect an explosion of some kind, but outwardly everything was as usual. At dusk the submarine surfaced cautiously, after a long search of the sea through the periscope. It was a calm, clear night. Small parties of the crew were allowed above decks, and when the boy's turn came he found the air warm and balmy, with a light, steady breeze blowing. He had been on deck perhaps fifteen minutes when a lookout in the conning tower called that land was in sight.

Barney stared into the gloom and made out a low, dark fringe of trees on the horizon to the south. Just then the bosun appeared at his shoulder. "Get below, you," he commanded roughly. "Stay in der bunk room. Und don't try noddings!"

The boy had no choice but to obey. He was alone in the crew's quarters when Grauner came in, a few minutes later.

"So Blohm chased you below," the big gunner grinned. "Scared you'd try to swim for it, maybe. But that wouldn't do you no good here."

"Why?" Barney asked him. "Where are we?"

Grauner looked around to make sure nobody was within hearing. "It's a little island east o' the Bahamas," he answered in a low voice. "Hangman's Cay, some say it's called. Nobody lived on it till the war. Now we got a pretty good base fixed up. The boats pull in there to paint their topsides white for duty in the Caribbean. That's so they can't be seen from the air when they're on sand bottom. There's a surgeon on the staff there, an' when Rasch reported the Captain was hurt he got orders to make for the island."

Barney was still very much awake an hour later, when the U-boat slowed down and approached the secret base. He could see nothing from where he lay in the bunk room but he could hear the commands and imagine what was happening. First the *Sea Snake* hove to and signaled with the blinker light. The boy figured there was an outer barrier reef around the island, and the submarine would have to identify herself before she was allowed to enter. After a few minutes an answering signal was reported to the control room and the engines were ordered quarter speed ahead.

Slowly the U-432 nosed her way in, with seamen in the bows calling soundings. Once inside the lagoon there was evidently deeper water. The ventilators brought down sounds from the deck. A distant voice hailed and was answered from aboard the submarine. Soon the engines were reversed and she was maneuvering into a berth of some kind. Cables thudded and a winch creaked as she was made fast. Then many feet came down the companion ladder. Through the door of the control room, Barney caught a glimpse of a strange officer in a white uniform. He was talking to Lieutenant Rasch as they headed aft toward the Captain's cabin. Four men carrying a stretcher followed them.

A few minutes later the group reappeared, and this time there was a heavy, inert figure on the stretcher. It took some time to hoist the Captain up through the conning-tower hatch. When they were gone a heavy silence settled over the vessel.

Barney was alone in the bunk room. He sat on the edge

of his berth and fidgeted for nearly an hour, then rose and walked quietly to the control room door. There was no one in sight there. He wondered if all the crew had been given liberty ashore. Blohm's orders were still fresh in his memory but it looked now as if the bosun had taken no steps to have him guarded.

Stepping lightly, the boy moved to the foot of the ladder and stood listening. Everything was quiet above. He waited with a quickening pulse while he counted to a hundred, then started to climb. There was no light in the conning tower. He paused just below the hatch till his eyes grew used to the darkness. When he could make sure that there was nobody above, he pulled himself up and peered out along the deck. A very dim, blue-shaded light shone on the gang-plank. There were no stars visible overhead, and after a moment he realized that the sky was hidden by a leaf-covered camou-flage net. The deck and the pier alongside were empty.

Barney drew a long breath. His chance of escape was a slim one, it was true—but even a sudden bullet might be better than a Nazi prison camp. His German sneakers made no noise on the deck. In half a dozen strides he had crossed over to the pier and was walking along it toward the land. He tried to go without hurrying, and he had time to notice how cleverly the base had been concealed. From the air the net over the submarine berth would appear to be ragged palm trees. The pier itself had an unused, dilapidated look, and at its shoreward end stood a small shanty that might be an abandoned fishing shack.

He was almost abreast of the tumble-down structure when a figure stepped from its doorway. In the faint starlight Barney could make out a uniform unlike those of the submarine crew. The man held a rifle and the bayonet glinted coldly.

"Halt!" came the gruff German voice. "You're the Yankee prisoner, *nicht wahr?*"

The word "Yankee" stung the Carolina boy and he was no longer frightened. "Not me!" he replied in German. Then he managed a fairly convincing chuckle. "You'll find the pig asleep in the bunk room. Which way do I go for a drink of beer?"

The guard grunted and slung the rifle on his shoulder by its strap. "Sorry," he said. "A natural mistake. I thought all of you were ashore. Not much beer left, but you'll find everybody at the canteen. Straight ahead up that path. *Heil Hitler!*"

Barney crossed his fingers and "heiled" in return. Then

he strolled on in the direction indicated by the German. He need hardly have asked the way, for sounds of singing and laughter came from the palm grove a few hundred feet from the shore.

The boy went on till he was in the thick darkness under the trees. There he turned quickly to the left and set off at right angles to the path. It was fairly open between the palm trunks, but the sand and coral were rough under his feet. He stumbled on for perhaps twenty paces. Then suddenly a low building of some kind barred his way. The wall he touched with his hands was made of a hard, scratchy material—coral blocks, he thought. The roof sloped back into the sand and the higher front of the building faced toward the lagoon. Overhead he could see the irregular outlines of camouflage on a net stretched between the trees.

Barney felt his way to the left and along the front of the structure. There were no windows, but he came to a wide wooden door, securely fastened. From the fact that it had been built so near the dock and so far from the canteen and other post buildings, he imagined it must be a storehouse for shells and torpedoes.

To make his progress easier the boy kept close to the shore but stayed within the shadow of the trees. It was hardly necessary to move quietly, for the steady breeze made a loud rustling in the palm fronds and small waves slapped in along the sand. When he had obeyed the sudden impulse to leave the submarine he had no plans, and for the first few minutes the joy of feeling dry land under his feet was enough. Now he began to have doubts. His one chance of escape seemed to be to find a hiding place on some remote part of the cay. Then, if there was any food to be had, he might hope to steal a small boat and reach a port in the Bahamas, not too many leagues to the westward.

To his dismay the beach curved constantly toward the right, and he soon realized that the island was much smaller than he had expected. Actually he was moving in a circle, a scant half mile in diameter. The fact was all too plain when he heard lusty German voices singing a beer-hall song a short distance ahead. He had made the round of the cay and was back almost at the point where he had started.

Panic took hold of him then. He stood shivering in the night wind. There was no place to hide. In any kind of organized search they would recapture him within half an hour.

Desperation made the boy turn back toward the lagoon. He crept down through the fringing palms and reached a tiny basin cut out of the coral. In the dim starlight that filtered through the camouflage net he could see the shadows of a launch and two smaller boats moored there, a few yards from the bank.

For a moment he hesitated, facing the almost hopeless odds that would be against him. No food, no chart, no sail. And if he succeeded in getting out through the reef without being seen by the pier guard he must run the chance of storms over an unknown stretch of sea. Nevertheless he could try. He clenched his teeth to stop their chattering and prepared to swim to the nearest boat. But before he could plunge into the water a footstep crunched the gravel just behind him and a hoarse whisper froze him in his tracks.

"Hold it, punk! Don't be a fool!"

# 11

THE paralysis of fear gripped Barney only a second or two. He whirled about and saw the huge figure of Grauner looming in the shadow. The gunner reached out a hand and seized his wrist. "Come back here before somebody sees you," he muttered. "How'd you get ashore?"

"I—I just walked past the guard," Barney whispered. "He thought I was one o' the crew."

"Hmm—well, I ain't blaming you for trying to get away. Only you wouldn't have as much chance as a snowball. Maybe there'll be another time. Right now I got to get you aboard again before Blohm comes back, or there'll be the devil to pay."

Still holding the boy's arm in his powerful grip, Grauner led the way back through the trees to the path. "Only way to get by that dumb guard," he whispered, "is for you to make out like you've had too much to drink. Don't open your trap. Just be pie-eyed an' stupid, see? I'm puttin' you back in your bunk."

They came slowly down the path toward the pierhead shack. Barney staggered and dragged his feet, and the gunner put an arm around him as if to support him.

"*Heil Hitler!*" the guard greeted them.

"*Sieg heil! Sieg heil!*" replied Grauner cheerfully. "The young Fritz, here, hasn't learned to hold good beer. He's a bit under the weather."

The man with the rifle laughed and went back into his shelter while they reeled on along the pier. There was no sign of life on the U-boat's deck. When they reached the shadow of the conning tower Grauner motioned Barney to stay where he was.

"I'll take a look below," he murmured. "If you hear me singing it's all right to come down."

During the few seconds that he stood there alone Barney debated the crazy idea of dropping overboard and swimming to the basin where the boats were moored. But his desperate resolve had weakened. Now that he knew Grauner was his friend, imprisonment on the submarine seemed more bearable. And as the gunner had so surprisingly told him, there might be another time for escape.

Up through the hatch came the bass rumble of a song—"*Du bist wie eine Blume*." Barney slipped inside and scrambled quickly down the ladder. When the crew returned, half an hour later, he was lying innocently in his bunk pretending to be asleep.

The men were noisy and quarrelsome after their brief shore leave. It was after midnight when their voices finally subsided into snores. The boy lay there thinking, unable at first to go to sleep. His position could be a lot worse, he realized. Foolishly he had risked giving away the fact that he could understand German, but as things had turned out nobody suspected it. By the accident of Grauner's finding him and bringing him back aboard, the guard need never know he had been talking to an American prisoner. As for the big ex-wrestler himself, Barney was both grateful and puzzled. He would be glad to have a powerful ally but he was still not sure how far he could trust him. For the time being he decided to wait and see what happened.

When the boy woke again it was to hear the call to quarters ringing out over the loudspeaker. Stupid with beer and sleep, the men stumbled out of their berths and pulled on their shoes. Some of them muttered curses and asked why they had to get up early on their first day in port. They soon had an answer. Blohm thrust his scowling face in at the door and bawled out a string of orders. All hands were to load ammunition and provisions. The U-boat would sail again as soon as darkness came.

The men stared at each other when the bosun was gone. Leaving so soon? What about the *Herr Kapitan?* And where would they be sent on patrol? A dozen conflicting ideas were offered but nobody appeared to know the truth. They went out growling and shaking their heads.

Barney was sitting on the edge of his bunk, alone in the room, when Blohm looked in again a few minutes later. "Go help der cook," he said. "Stay dere as long as he needs you. Und don't try to go on deck."

The cook was still sleepy and grumpy after his evening ashore. He sat on his stool in the galley and let Barney do the work of preparing breakfast. At the end of an hour the meal was ready and the men filed past to get their rations. Grauner was back near the end of the line. As he came by, the scarred lid of one of his squinty eyes flickered in a solemn wink. It was a reassuring sign that the boy's attempt to escape had not been discovered, and he was thankful for it.

As soon as the meal was done he was put to work washing dishes. Men were passing constantly, carrying shells, boxes of ammunition and supplies of all kinds. A few cases of food were added to the dwindling pile in the storeroom, and Barney saw some drums of lubricating oil taken aft.

He was just finishing his task when young Hans came stumbling by, along the passage. He was clutching a round metal can that looked both heavy and slippery. Right behind him hurried the Chief Engineer.

"Watch it, you clumsy lubber!" the officer bellowed. "Don't drop that—"

He was too late with the warning. Hans tripped and the container went skittering out of his arms. Instinctively Barney ducked and flung up an elbow to shield his head. He expected a terrific explosion. But after the clatter made by the can on the deck plates there was no sound except Hans' panting whimper.

"I—I didn't mean to drop it, sir! I—it slipped!"

"Be still, you fool!" snapped the engineer. "We've got to save as much of it as we can or we'll never get home. Here—cook—give us a cup or something, quick!"

Barney stuck his head into the passage and saw a scattered heap of grayish brown powder. Hastily he seized two metal cups from the rack and gave one to the angry officer. With the other in his hand he knelt down and began scooping up the spilled material, whatever it was.

"Be careful with that," cautioned the officer. "We don't know how it would work if there was any dirt in it."

Then he glanced up at Barney and frowned. "Oh," he said. "You don't understand German. You'd better keep out of this. Go on—go away!" And there was no mistaking his gesture of dismissal.

Barney went back into the galley, where the cook was taking one of his frequent naps. Looking down at the cup he was still holding, the boy saw some of the gray powder in the bottom. He was about to throw it out, but something stayed his hand. Thoughtfully he reached in his pocket and pulled out his water-proof match-safe—one of the few belongings they had allowed him to keep. He unscrewed the top and poured the powder carefully in. There was only about a teaspoonful of it but he thought it was worth saving. When the metal box was tightly fastened and wrapped in its oilskin covering, he returned it to his pocket.

Outside, in the passageway, the engineer and his hapless helper had nearly finished refilling the can. "Let's see," Barney heard the officer say. "Thirty kilograms—and we've saved a good four-fifths of it. Hmm—well, that's all there is on the island. We'll have to make it last."

They put the cover on and Hans lifted the can gingerly once more. The last Barney saw of them they were moving through the crew's quarters toward the engine room.

The loading of supplies was completed in a few hours, and when Barney had finished his work in the galley after the noon meal he found the men in the bunk room grumbling and gossiping. As usual they paid no attention to him but went right on talking as he slipped into his berth.

There was a considerable difference of opinion as to where they would cruise next. One faction held that the convoys along the coast were too well guarded now and they were likely to be sent south into the Caribbean. Others scoffed at the idea.

"You'd be out on the hull with a brush and a bucket of white paint right now if we were headed that way," Froelich argued. "There's better hunting off the African coast these days. I tell you we'll be making a course southeast."

Young Hans, usually silent in the fo'c'sle counsels, swallowed once or twice and offered a timid opinion. "I think maybe we're going home," he announced, blushing.

They turned to stare at him. "You mean you *wish* we

were," jeered Froelich.

Hans shook his head. "It's not just wishing," he said. "This morning I dropped a can of the Chief Engineer's chemicals and he gave me a terrible dressing down. But when we'd gathered the stuff up he said he thought there was still enough to get us home."

"So!" growled one of the other seamen angrily. "And if there isn't enough, it will be your fault. When the engines stop we'll throw you overboard and let you swim ashore!"

"What about it, Hans?" Grauner's deep voice rumbled. "You work in the engine room. How many kilometers can we travel on one of those cans of chemicals?"

The youth twisted his red hands in embarrassment. "I wish I knew," he sighed, "but I'm not very sharp about those things. The Chief says it's all still a secret."

Barney, listening eagerly to all that was said, felt his hopes sink. Whether they were bound for Africa or Germany, his chances of escape seemed to be approaching the vanishing point. For the moment he wished miserably that Grauner had left him alone the night before. Even now he might be making his try for freedom. But the conversation gave him other things to think about as well.

He had had a half-formed suspicion, ever since the powder was spilled in the passageway, that it might have some connection with the fuel mystery. And everything Hans and the others said strengthened his idea. It was possible he had all the pieces of the puzzle before him now—if he only knew how to fit them together!

The crew was given supper early that night, in preparation for their departure. Barney was just putting away the last of the washed utensils when a voice rasped over the loud-speaker system. "All hands will come immediately to the control room to hear an announcement by the commanding officer."

The rotund cook got off his stool, panting and sighing, and waddled forward with Barney in his wake. Men from the after bunk room pressed behind them, and soon the entire personnel of the ship was wedged into the narrow space around the periscope shafts.

"What's it all about? . . . Who is the commanding officer, anyhow? . . . Maybe we'll learn where we're going," the seamen murmured.

Lieutenant Rasch had been ashore with the officers of the base all day. Now he appeared on the conning-tower ladder, his face flushed and his eyes bright. He paused on the second rung above the deck, looking around at the close-packed group below him. There was an arrogance in his bearing that stirred Barney's hate.

Suddenly the Lieutenant flung up his arm stiffly. *"Heil Hitler!"* he cried, and the words rang back with a harsh, derisive sound from the steel bulkheads.

"I have an announcement to make," the young officer declaimed. "Because of an unfortunate accident to Captain Von Sturm, he will be unable to continue the voyage. I have been placed in command of our ship. From this moment I expect unfaltering obedience and loyalty from every man aboard. My orders are secret but I can tell you that the U-432 has an opportunity to bring deathless glory to the name of our noble Fuehrer! *Heil Hitler!* We will sail in twenty minutes. Disperse!"

The men were silent for a moment, then answered with a scattered chorus of "heils" before pushing their way forward and aft. There was a lot of whispering and head-shaking going on in the bunk room when Barney got there. Most of the crew were troubled by what they had heard. A few made wild guesses as to the mission at which Rasch had hinted, but all were agreed it didn't sound like a voyage home.

Shortly the call to stations was sounded. The engines

began to throb and the submarine was backed gently out of her berth under the camouflage net. Cruising on the surface at quarter-speed, and with the leadsmen taking soundings every few seconds, she crept across the lagoon and found the opening in the outer reef.

Barney knew all this by sound and feel, for Blohm had not yet given him permission to leave his quarters. All the rest of the men were on deck or at work in other parts of the vessel and he sat alone in his bunk, deep in a fit of the blues. What devilment was Rasch planning against his country? he wondered miserably. Something extra daring if he could judge from the glitter in the young Nazi officer's eyes. And he himself would be helpless to do anything about it.

Gradually the vibration of the Diesels quickened and the *Sea Snake* picked up cruising speed. He could picture her ugly black snout thrusting through the waves and the water creaming back along her lean flanks. There was a sea running outside, he judged, for the submarine had begun to pitch and heave. He waited what seemed a long time for the crew to come below. Finally they came straggling in. One of the last to appear was the gigantic gunner. He yawned, stretched and grinned down at the Carolina boy.

"Had a little fresh air and a smoke, anyway," he said.

"Tasted good."

"Tell me," Barney whispered. "What course are we on?"

"North," said Grauner. "Due north. If we keep going, we'll run smack into your old hang-out 'round Cape Hatteras!"

# 12

ONCE or twice in the night the boy woke restlessly. He could feel the strong thrust of the motors and the uneasy motion of the ship that told him they were still running on the surface. When the watch was changed at dawn the order came to submerge, and the depth gauge showed ten meters when the submarine leveled out. Rasch kept her moving northward under water all morning, sending up the periscope for a look around every few minutes.

Barney was in the bunk room sometime near midafternoon when he heard the Lieutenant's shout, shrill with excitement. "Call all hands—battle stations! I've got a small sailing vessel in sight, not four kilometers ahead. Stand by to surface!"

The men went to their allotted places but Barney thought

they moved with somewhat less alacrity than in the days under Captain Von Sturm. Rasch must have noticed it, too, for he called the bosun angrily and gave him a cursing for their slowness.

The U-boat rose smoothly enough and was cutting along through the waves with her decks awash.

"Gun crew on deck!" snapped the Lieutenant. "Come— lively there, Grauner! I want to get this job done and get under again."

Barney could not see the big gunner's face from where he stood inside the bunk room door, but he could imagine the scowl on those battered features. There was a sound of feet mounting the rungs of the companion ladder. Rasch was about to follow the men up when he spied the American boy.

"Ah," he said, in his affected English, "our young guest! I think it might be instructive for you to see what is about to happen. A little lesson in Nazi efficiency. Up with you!"

For an instant Barney was too astonished to move, but in response to the officer's impatient gesture he hurried to the ladder and scrambled up. Rasch was right behind him when he reached the conning tower.

"Outside, on deck," the Lieutenant ordered. "Keep clear

of the gun crew."

It was a cloudy afternoon, with a dark threat of rain banking up astern and a fresh breeze blowing off the port beam. The narrow gray-black deck still glistened with water, though only the spray from the wave tops now came aboard.

A point or two on the starboard bow Barney could see a small two-masted schooner wallowing along close-hauled. Her canvas was weathered gray and she appeared to be flying no flag of any kind. She was about two miles away and sailing on the same course as the submarine.

Before him the crew had already stripped off the covering of the five-inch gun and were busily swabbing the breech block and firing mechanism. A rack of shells had been sent up through the ammunition hatch and lay ready at hand.

"Good enough," came Grauner's bass growl. "Load the gun." One of the long shells was slapped home and the breech closed with a muffled click. The gunner bent his huge shoulders and sighted along the grim gray barrel. His hands were busy with the wheels that turned the swivel and raised or lowered the muzzle. After a moment he seemed to be satisfied, for he turned and looked questioningly at the conning tower.

Rasch had climbed to the tiny "bridge," ten feet above

the deck. He was watching the other vessel through a pair of powerful binoculars.

"Just another of those island schooners," he announced with contempt. "Hold your fire, there. You'll have better use for those shells later. Wait till we're close enough to do it with one shot."

Grauner shrugged and turned to stare at the little sailing ship. She was being rapidly overhauled, for the submarine was making a surface speed of close to twenty knots.

When they had come up within half a mile, there was a flutter of canvas aboard the schooner and she swung her blunt bows into the wind. Frightened by the chase, the men aboard her had decided to heave to and wait.

"Want me to signal her, sir?" asked the young junior officer on the bridge.

"No," grunted the Lieutenant. "I'll give the orders. You wait for them."

"Yes, sir," Barney heard the other man murmur apologetically. The U-boat churned along on her course and the gun crew stood silent, staring forward. Grauner's feet shifted restlessly but he did not look again at the tower.

Waiting there, the boy felt a cold sweat break out on his forehead. If Rasch had wanted to torture him he was accomplishing his purpose. There was something deadly in the submarine's advance. Her speed had been cut down now but the schooner was barely two hundred yards off. Barney could see four or five black, frightened faces along her taffrail.

The tension finally grew too great. One of the schooner's men flung up his arm. "What you want, Mistuh?" he screamed. "We ain' got no boat!"

Rasch leaned on the bridge rail. "Gunner," he said, "you may fire now. See what you can do with one shell—amidships."

Stolidly Grauner trained the gun for point-blank range and the deck leaped to the crashing discharge. Almost instantly the shell exploded and the little wooden vessel seemed to disintegrate before their eyes. Huge fragments of her deck and side planking rose in the air, and the mainmast, blown clean out of her, fell into the sea in a tangle of rigging. Barney saw at least one grotesque black figure tossed high by the explosion, but nothing moved aboard her after the debris had fallen. There was a great gaping hole in her side and she was settling fast by the stern.

The boy shuddered and was starting to turn away when he saw a head bobbing on the waves. One of the Negroes

was swimming toward the submarine, his arms thrashing the water with long, desperate strokes. Rasch had seen him, too. His voice came now from the conning tower.

"Grauner—go aft to the machine gun."

The big man had been methodically cleaning the forward gun while the crew returned the shells to the magazine. He turned at the words and stared at the Lieutenant, his ugly mouth set in a tight, grim line. For two or three tense seconds he did not move. Then, so deliberately that every step was an insult, he started to stroll aft.

Rasch's plump face was purple with fury. He whirled and shouted toward the stern. "You, Froelich—uncover the machine gun and take care of that fellow in the water. Grauner, get below and stay in your quarters!"

The giant gunner passed Barney without a glance and disappeared through the hatch. The boy could have seen the machine gun by moving a step or two toward the guard rail, but he could not take his eyes off the swimmer. There was stark terror on the man's contorted face and his eyeballs rolled wildly.

"He'p me, Mistuh!" he shrieked. "They's sharks aftuh me!" With a shiver the boy saw a curved gray fin cutting a narrowing circle in the water around the Negro. There was a life-preserver ring fastened to the front of the conning tower and Barney made a leap for it. But while his shaky hands fumbled with the lashings he heard the ripping sound of machine-gun fire. Two short bursts. And when he turned his head, the swimmer was gone.

Sick with horror, Barney stumbled to the hatch and groped his way down to the bunk room. What he had seen was cold-blooded murder.

He did not know just what time it was when they came for Grauner. He had fallen into a troubled sleep shortly after the U-boat submerged. Suddenly an ominous voice close to his bunk woke him with a start. There were three men standing there in the narrow aisle—Blohm and two others—and they were all armed.

The bosun had a big automatic pistol in his hand. "Come with us and come quietly," he ordered.

Barney heard the big gunner grunt softly overhead. Then his legs appeared as he let himself down from the berth. He yawned and stretched his massive arms and grinned down at Blohm. "Put the gun away," he said. "I'll come with you."

The other men in the bunk room watched in silence while the bosun's squad marched their prisoner aft. Even after the door closed nobody spoke. There was a heavy, unnatural quiet in the place, as if each man feared and distrusted his neighbors. "Like convicts in a jail-house," thought Barney with a shiver.

He was glad when it was time to go to the galley, for any kind of work was better than sitting still and remembering. While he sliced black bread and made soup he wondered what was happening to Grauner. The man's action had come very close to mutiny, and discipline was harsh in Nazi ships. On the other hand he was credited with being one of the best gunners in the U-boat service. If he could keep his temper under the tongue-lashing Rasch was sure to give him there was a chance he might be let off with no worse punishment than a few days in the brig.

Barney remembered the brig. He had noticed it the first time he visited the stern torpedo compartment. The tiny cell was not more than three feet by five, with a slotted steel door and a heavy lock. He had peered in and imagined himself a prisoner there. It was bare except for a metal stool built into one corner. There was no bed of any kind, no sanitary arrangements. For a man of Grauner's huge proportions the cramped space would be a torture chamber.

It was while the boy was bent over the stove with his

back to the galley door that heavy feet tramped past along the passage. "Heh-heh!" the cook chuckled maliciously. "So we'll have one less big stomach to feed for a while!"

Barney glanced around but he was too late to see the men pass. He drew his own conclusion from the cook's remark, however. It must have been Blohm's squad taking Grauner aft.

Soon the meal was ready and the men off watch were called on the loudspeaker. They marched by and received their rations in sullen silence. After they had finished the watch was changed and those who had been on duty were fed. Barney looked at each man in turn, but the giant gunner was not among them.

While the boy was still cleaning up in the galley the steward from the officers' mess arrived with an armful of dirty dishes. The man paused a moment, picking his teeth and exchanging a few pleasantries with the cook. "Oh, by the way," he said at last, "the *Herr Leutnant* ordered that something be given the prisoner in the brig. No hurry—and nothing fancy, I should say. A pan of water and a chunk of bread if you have any that's hard and stale. That ought to keep our tame gorilla alive for a day! Ha-ha!"

The cook's fat paunch shook with laughter. "Better still,"

he replied, "I have an old piece with green mold on it. Just the kind of rich food he tells us about eating in that accursed America! *Heil Hitler!*"

"*Heil Hitler!*" the steward replied with a salute, and departed grinning.

The cook turned on Barney. "Ven you are done," he growled, "gif dis to Grauner." And he picked a particularly nasty-looking heel of black bread out of the garbage bucket.

The boy shuddered. "Where is he?" he asked, pretending he did not know.

The cook pointed a greasy thumb aft. "Go in der torpedo room," he said. "You find him. Gif some wasser, too."

Barney filled a pannikin with water, took the moldy bread and went along the passage, through the engine room and into the torpedo compartment. Closing the door behind him, he looked around. There was nobody in sight.

"Hiya, punk!" The low voice came through the slots of the cell door.

"Hi," Barney whispered. "They sent me with some water and this dirty piece of bread. The cook was watching, but next time I'll try to fetch along something fit to eat."

He shoved the bread and water through a small opening at the bottom of the door.

Grauner gave a grunt of disgust as the faint light fell on the unappetizing food. "That cook—the low-down pig!" he muttered in English. "Him an' a couple of others has always had it in for me. Oh, well, I can live a while on next to nothin'. An' if I ever get out o' this here hole I'm goin' to bust a few heads."

"What did the Lieutenant say?" Barney breathed.

"Plenty!" The gunner was grim. "Told me if he had me ashore I'd go to concentration camp. You better chase along, bub, or somebody'll think it's funny you're stayin' so long."

Barney took the hint and left at once. Two or three men glanced up at him as he went through the engine room but he didn't think the time he had spent with Grauner had been long enough to cause any comment. When he got to the officers' quarters he saw Froelich entering the Captain's cabin. The door closed quickly but as he passed he could catch the sound of the man's obsequious voice addressing the *"Herr Kapitan-Leutnant."*

Something about that voice reminded the boy of that night on the southward cruise when he had heard Froelich and Grauner whispering. It had been Froelich, he remembered, who hinted at foul play in the case of the injured Captain. And now the fellow was playing up to Rasch—

fairly licking his boots. Maybe he had been wrong in think-ing Froelich was on the side of those who hated the Nazi Lieutenant. At any rate the man would bear watching.

Barney was not sent aft with food for his big friend again that day, and he could invent no excuse for a visit to the brig without orders. The U-boat surfaced soon after dark-ness fell. The moment she stuck her nose out of water she began to pitch and roll, and old hands in the bunk room shook their heads. "No deck liberty tonight," they told each other. "There's a storm out there."

Sure enough, when the lookout came down from the con-ning tower at the end of the watch, he reported wind and rain and a heavy sea running. "She's making plenty of kilo-meters northward though," he added. "The storm's coming up from astern and pushing us along."

Barney lay back in his bunk and tried to do some mental dead reckoning. He figured it must be seven or eight hun-dred miles from Hangman's Cay to Hatteras if he recalled his father's old coastal charts correctly. Traveling on the surface the submarine could log as much as two hundred miles in the ten hours between dark and dawn. Even at her lower submerged speed she would probably add another hundred and forty miles in fourteen hours of under-water cruising. If she didn't loiter along the way to attack any ships, and if she wasn't forced to seek safety on the bottom, another thirty-six hours would put her in his own home waters off the Carolina coast! Rocked by the long heave of the roaring sea he went to sleep, and in a few moments he was dreaming of a sunny day's fishing aboard the *Jennie May*.

# 13

THE gale was still blowing when morning came, and the seas had risen to such proportions that the U-boat was running submerged. Barney heard a helmsman talking about it before breakfast. The man had come down from the conning tower about midnight, battered and drenched.

"You wouldn't believe it," he said, "but we were logging thirty kilometers there for a while—and more than that up and down! I never heard such a wind! It was a lucky thing for all of us when the *Herr Leutnant* finally ordered her taken under."

Even at a depth of seventy-five feet, where the submarine was now cruising, the upheaval above caused uneasy motions and tremors in the tough steel hull.

Barney worked in the galley till the midday meal had

been served and the cleaning-up finished. Watching the sleepy cook he managed to smuggle a few scraps of food into his pockets. When all the other chores were done he turned to the cook with a casual question.

"Bread and water for the prisoner?" he asked, trying to keep any hint of eagerness out of his voice.

"Ya," the fat man grunted, pointing to a stale crust he had laid aside. "Dot vill make him happy!" And he gave one of his unpleasant, wheezy chuckles.

The boy filled a pan with water, took the bread and went aft. Luck was with him again for he found nobody at work in the torpedo room.

"How you making out?" he asked Grauner in a whisper as he knelt by the door of the brig.

"Lousy!" groaned the big gunner. "I got cramps in me legs an' arms, not bein' able to stretch out. Hey! What's this? Real grub for a change!"

"I swiped it from the galley," Barney explained. "They'd skin me if they knew. How long you reckon they aim to keep you in here?"

"Till they need me, topside. Listen, kid. Don't say nothin' in front of that guy Froelich. I should have spotted him before I shot off my big mouth. *Gestapo*—that's what he is,

Planted in the fo'c'sle to trap us into talkin'. Rasch had heard what I said about him an' the Captain an' that's why he was layin' for me. It's time for you to be gettin' along. Here's the old water pan."

Barney picked up the empty tin and took it forward. He saw Froelich idling in the control room and wondered whether the man was really watching him or whether he only imagined it. Grauner's warning was hardly unexpected. It fitted perfectly with his own suspicions. If he valued his hide it behooved him to keep a weather eye on the Nazi spy.

By nightfall the storm had passed over and the submarine was able to surface, though mountainous seas were still running. That was the roughest night the boy had experienced since he had been aboard. He wasn't seasick but he had to grip the sides of his berth to keep from being thrown out.

The motion eased somewhat before morning. At daylight the U-432 submerged once more and plowed along steadily under water until a few minutes past noon. Barney was in the galley when he heard the engines stop. His heart beat faster in the heavy, unaccustomed silence. They must have reached their destination, wherever that might be.

Again that afternoon the boy visited the brig with food and water for his friend, but this time there were other men

in the torpedo compartment and they had no chance to ex-
change words. He thought Grauner must be really suffering,
for the big man smothered a grunt of pain when he reached
down to take the water pan.

Through the hours until dark the ship lay on bottom like
a sleeping shark. The depth gauge registered sixty meters,
so Barney knew they had come into fairly shoal water. There
was a restless expectancy among the crew. Some of the older
hands in the bunk room offered guesses about what was
going to happen but nobody seemed certain.

A little after sunset the engines began to throb again and
the submarine went up to periscope depth before surfacing.
Soon the radio man came into the control room and began
sending. The broken buzz of *dit—darr* made a nervous background for the talk in the crew's quarters. Barney knew a
little Morse but he could understand no word of the message. It would be in code, of course.

For three hours the U-boat lay rocking on the long
ground swells, her engines silent. No deck liberty was
granted, but a double lookout was kept on watch above.
Barney, far from being sleepy, lay in his bunk and listened.
After a long time he thought he caught the sound he was
waiting for. He laid his ear to the plates of the inner hull and

sure enough there was a faint, distant throbbing.

The vibration must have been picked up some time before by the submarine's listening devices, for there was a stir of activity in the control room. Lieutenant Rasch and the second officer climbed to the conning tower. Soon a muffled hail came down from the open hatch. There was a scurry of feet overhead and then a slight scraping sound along the side of the hull.

Barney leaned on one elbow and waited, watching the control room and the steel ladder. He was so sure of what he was going to see that the sudden appearance of a man in civilian clothes coming down the companionway was no surprise to him. The bulky figure was that of his old acquaintance—the owner of Caldee Castle.

Rasch followed immediately and Barney could see the young officer strutting, even in the cramped quarters of the control room. He was doing the honors of the ship in real quarterdeck style.

"Come aft to my cabin, Herr Ohlgren," the Lieutenant invited his guest. "I have a few bottles of fairly good wine, and we'll drink a toast or two while the supplies are brought aboard. I've been given orders for a mission that ought to interest you. We'll be free to talk, back here."

With that he led the way into the passage, and Barney heard no more. A couple of the seamen grinned at each other. "There ought to be some food fit to eat for a few days, anyway," one remarked.

"Ya," replied the other. "And if the steward keeps his ears open, maybe we'll find out something about this secret mission the *Herr Leutnant* is so proud of."

Ohlgren remained closeted with the *Sea Snake's* commander for more than an hour, and it was nearing midnight when word was passed to the watch on deck to call the *Valkyr* alongside once more.

The two men were flushed and smiling as they came from the cabin. "It should be a great occasion," Barney heard Ohlgren say. "I wish you all success, and it would be a pleasure to go with you. However, I must keep up appearances here if I'm to do my duty for the Fuehrer. *Heil Hitler!*"

"*Heil Hitler!*" Rasch clicked his heels and saluted smartly before he ushered the big man up the ladder.

Barney gritted his teeth as he rolled over in the bunk to go to sleep. It was maddening to know that the traitor Ohlgren was still free to carry on his work of supplying the U-boats. Many times the boy had comforted himself with the assurance that the whole Caldee gang must be languishing in prison or facing execution. He wondered what had gone wrong. Surely Slug Martin would have known what his disappearance meant and started an investigation. Tired and angry, he vowed to himself before he fell asleep that if he ever succeeded in getting ashore he would put Ohlgren and his Nazi followers behind bars.

*　　*　　*

In the morning he found the submarine's larder had been replenished with several hundred cans of food—meats, vegetables and fruit juices that bore good American brands. It fairly made his mouth water just to read the labels.

The steward saw him looking into the store closet and scowled.

"Not for der men!" he shook his head. "Dot iss for der officers' mess."

And so it turned out. The meals he helped prepare in the galley that day were the same unsavory stuff as before. The crew grumbled and cursed when they saw what they were served.

"It wasn't like this when the *Herr Kapitan* was aboard," Barney heard one man mutter to his neighbor. "We got a taste of the good things at least."

The U-boat had resumed her voyage in the night and all that day she continued steadily northward below the surface. Apparently she was headed for a new hunting ground, perhaps off the Delaware Capes or the port of New York.

After the meal at noon Barney filled a water pan and asked the cook what else he should give the prisoner. The man's fat paunch jiggled with mirth as he fished something out of the garbage. The officers had dined on roast lamb, and what the cook held up was the bone, stripped of everything but a few small shreds of meat and gristle.

"Let der big dog chew on it," he chuckled.

Fortunately Barney had some pieces of bread in his pockets as well. He took the bone without comment and started aft. As he opened the door into the passageway leading to the engine room he saw that the panel in the port bulkhead was standing ajar. That was the one he had once tried to open and found locked! He walked past as slowly as he dared and looked in. The space was nearly filled by a huge retort of stainless steel or some other shiny metal. Standing beside it, just inside the door, was the chief engineer. He glanced up quickly as the boy passed and his face wore a startled frown. With his left hand he was lifting the lid of a kind of metal hopper on the side of the retort. In his right, he held a graduated glass beaker like those Barney had seen in the high-school chemistry laboratory at home. And the beaker was filled nearly to the brim with grayish-brown powder!

The boy turned his head away hastily and hurried on, almost spilling the water in his excitement. He was positive that the chemical the engineer was about to pour into the retort was the same material he had helped to scoop up from the floor of the passage, that day at Hangman's Cay.

There were two men in the engine room, but when he passed through into the torpedo compartment he was glad to find it empty.

"That you, punk?" came a hoarse whisper from the steel cage in the corner.

"Yes," Barney answered. "How are you getting on?"

"Ugh!" The husky groan was answer enough.

The boy pushed the food and water through into the cell and told Grauner what the cook had said about the bone.

"All I ask is a chance to get at that pot-bellied skunk!" growled the gunner. "I'd give all the dough I ever made in the ring to have him by the neck right now."

"You were right about our heading for Hatteras," Barney told the prisoner. "Maybe you heard that speed-boat come alongside last night. Same one that brought me aboard."

"So?" Grauner interrupted his munching. "An' where are we bound now?"

"Nor'east by north, last I heard. That ought to put us off New York tomorrow. I've got to go now. So long!"

Carrying the empty water pan he threaded his way back between the roaring engines with a curious look at those fuel pipes that came through the forward bulkhead. In the passageway, the door at the left had been closed once more, and the engineer officer was gone. But the brief glimpse Barney had had made him feel that he was right on the edge of solving his puzzle. He wanted to get off somewhere by himself and think it out.

Blohm saw him going through the control room and called him to polish brasswork. That kept him busy until time to get supper in the galley, and it was nearly eight o'clock when he was free to go to his berth.

As he passed the officers' quarters, Rasch's voice came through the partly open door of the cabin. He was giving an order to the bosun. "Get him out of there at once, but keep him under a close guard. Let him walk and stretch to get the cramps out of his legs. Then you'd better rout out the cook and give him some real food. We're less than a hundred and fifty kilometers from our objective now, and we want him ready to do some expert shooting an hour or two after midnight."

Barney's heart gave a jump. There was only one person they could be talking about—his big friend in the brig. He loitered till Blohm came out and saw him.

"Here, you!" ordered the bosun. "Back to der galley und make some supper—anyding you got—for one man."

That was what the boy had been hoping for. He jumped to the task with alacrity. The cook had already gone to his bunk and he had the galley to himself. He filled a big pan with water and dehydrated stew, and broke open a package of dried apples for an extra treat. It was a better meal than he had eaten himself, but he had an idea the huge gunner was close to starvation.

Five minutes later he heard a tramp of feet in the passage. Two armed guards appeared and shambling after them on wobbly legs was the gorilla-like figure of the one-time wrestler.

Grauner blinked and stared, half blinded in the bright light. His forehead was wrinkled by a scowl of hate as he searched the galley with his little pig eyes. "Where's that so-and-so of a cook?" he growled huskily.

"Never mind the cook," the bosun snapped. "If you know what's good for you, you'll keep your mouth shut and obey orders. Keep walking. Stretch those legs. Your supper'll be ready in a little while."

As he stirred the stew on the electric range, Barney watched them march the big fellow back and forth along the passage. It was pitiful to see how weak he was at first. But as the minutes went by his great back straightened and his tree-trunk legs moved with more assurance.

"All right," the boy announced. "Come and get it."

The guards let Grauner sit down on the cook's stool and Barney filled his plate with stew and black bread. He did not look at the boy who served him, but started shoveling in mighty mouthfuls of food.

When he had finished, he drank down half a gallon of water and wiped his mouth on the back of a hairy hand. "Well?" his deep voice rumbled. "What do you want of me now?"

"Come on forward," Blohm answered. "You'll get a few hours to stretch out in your bunk before we go into action."

The giant said nothing but rose and went into the passage, his shoulders filling the space between the bulkheads. As soon as Barney had washed and dried the dishes, he followed. The bosun's final words were ringing loud in his head. "A few hours . . . before we go into action." It was coming, then. The mission that had filled Lieutenant Rasch's thoughts since the night they left Hangman's Cay.

He shivered a little as he started through the control room. Blohm was standing there by the door to the crew's quarters, waiting for him. "*Der Herr Leutnant* asks to see you in his cabin," he told the boy coldly.

# 14

BARNEY had learned to fear and hate the fanatical young commander of the U-432. He had a feeling that the order to report to the cabin meant trouble, and he went aft with dragging feet. Rasch's voice answered when he knocked.

"Yes. Come in. And close the door after you."

The tiny room was so brightly lighted it made the boy blink for a moment. The Lieutenant sat stiffly at his desk, wearing the immaculate uniform that was a religion with him. His smooth cheeks were flushed a deeper pink than usual and his eyes held a glitter of excitement. He looked like a man in a fever.

He stared at Barney for several seconds as if he relished the sight of his visitor's uneasiness. "All right," he said at length, "you may sit."

With a deliberate gesture he lighted a cigarette and blew out a leisurely puff of smoke. "It is really a pleasure," he began, in his too-precise English, "to have an American guest aboard tonight. Even such a poor specimen of the breed as yourself. You will have an opportunity to see what war with the Reich means. And you will, I think, see a great many of your silly countrymen die."

He puffed again on the cigarette and smiled at the shocked look on the boy's face. "I will tell you something that is known only to the Second Officer and myself, of all the men aboard this ship."

To emphasize his words he leaned forward and Barney noticed that the hand holding the cigarette shook a little.

"As I told you once," he continued, "I was more fortunate than yourself in my opportunities for travel in your country. One of the journeys I made as a guest of those foolish Yankees was to a great seaside resort known as Atlantic City. It may be that in your provincial ignorance you have never heard of it. But I can tell you as much as you need to know.

"Atlantic City made me a better Nazi. Faugh! What a place! Great, gaudy hotels like Moorish palaces, twenty— thirty stories high. Blazing lights of every color. Amusement piers built out over the sea. And everywhere—on the promenades, on the sand and in the water—filthy, pushing crowds of Americans! Fat women wearing jewels, riding in wheelchairs. Loud-talking men with cigars in their mouths. Money —pleasure—selfishness. A degenerate people who deserve to be slaves!

"But what has all this to do with us, tonight? Look at the chart."

He rose and pointed to the big sea-map on the bulkhead behind him. The coast from Hatteras to Montauk was sharply drawn, with soundings, buoys and secret markings in German script. Rasch's finger stabbed at a point on the New Jersey shoreline.

"There is Atlantic City," he said. "And here"—the finger moved down and to the right—"is our approximate position at this minute."

The place he indicated was off the Delaware Capes, some sixty miles southeast of the resort town.

"You see," Rasch smiled, settling back in his chair, "I was an observant lad. The photographs I took and the questions I asked were useful to our files in Berlin. It was interesting to notice that the ambitious architects had built those great hotels as close to the ocean as possible. New York has a loftier skyline, but New York is guarded by forts and mine-fields, and its skyscrapers are anchored in rock. This imita-tion of Manhattan has sand for its foundation. And it stands only a few meters from the open beach.

"That, in itself, would make this playground of Americans a tempting target. But now see how your stupid government plays into our hands. From our agents we learn that all the immense hotels are now full of nice young soldiers, in train-ing. No doubt some of them may be the very brats who laughed at me for being German! I have thought of my revenge for six years. Tonight I will have it in full measure —and all to the glory of the Fuehrer! *Heil Hitler!*"

He seemed to have forgotten Barney as he snapped erect in the Nazi salute. His eyes at that moment were fixed and staring like those of a maniac. When he came back to reality he looked at the boy and frowned. The intoxication of his mood was gone. "Go," he snapped peevishly. "Go back to your berth and think of what I have said. I want you on deck when it happens—on deck, where you can see the fires and the destruction. Be there!"

Barney stumbled out and returned to the bunk room. All hands had turned in and there was little talking in the dimly lighted compartment. He crawled into his bunk and lay there shivering. A lot of things were clear to him now. This plan of the Lieutenant's to shell a big town from the sea didn't seem so crazy when he thought about it. It was just the kind of reckless stunt he would expect from Rasch, but it would hardly be allowed by the German navy unless it had a good chance of success.

Barney had seen a picture post-card of Atlantic City once, and he remembered how those huge, ornate buildings rose almost out of the blue sea. Grauner's deadly marksmanship and the U-boat's five-inch shells could do a lot of damage to those hotels. And if they were actually filled with sleeping soldiers, as Rasch said—the thought of it made his blood run cold.

For three hours the boy tossed and dozed fitfully. Then Blohm came in quietly and woke several of the men, telling them to follow him. It was another thirty minutes before the call to general quarters sounded and the bright lights were turned on. Growling as usual at having their sleep broken, the seamen turned out and went to their stations.

Grauner got up with the rest. He said nothing to Barney, but as he stood there by the berth putting on his deck clothes, his big hand slipped down and gave the boy's shoulder a gentle pat.

Remembering Rasch's parting order, Barney also prepared to go above. He had been given an old sweater which he pulled on over his German undershirt and dungarees. His bare feet shuffled into a pair of sneakers and he was ready to go on deck when the time came.

The submarine was still at periscope depth and from the soft throb of the engines he thought she was moving at only about quarter-speed. The control room was full of tense-faced men. The Lieutenant himself was at the periscope.

Minutes dragged by and there was no conversation. The sailors at the controls moved smartly in answer to occasional brief orders, but their watchful eyes were always on the stiff-backed young commander in the center of the cramped space.

At last he ceased his shifting of the periscope handles and they could see his shoulders tighten as he steadied the eye-piece. "Quartermaster," he called, without looking up, "change your course three points west."

"Yes, sir, three points west."

"Surfacing stations. We'll take her up gradually. Engines at dead slow."

"Yes, sir. All hands stand by to surface!"

The throb of the Diesels grew still more quiet as the men

jumped to their posts. The surfacing planes were tilted a little at a time, and the depth gauge indicator barely moved as the submarine rose inch by inch.

Rasch straightened and turned to his junior officer with a smile of satisfaction that all could see. "Keep all hands at stations," he said. "Be ready to dive instantly if I give the command. I want only the gun crew on deck—the gun crew and the young Yankee here. The signal from the shore is right. All is ready for our attack. This will be a proud night for Germany and for the Fuehrer. *Heil Hitler!*"

With that fanatical salute he stepped briskly to the companion and started upward. The sailor at the top turned the valve that opened the hatch. The crew of the gun followed their commander up the ladder, and Barney, prodded by the scowling bosun, was the last to make the climb.

Once out of the conning tower and on the wet, black deck, the boy needed a moment to adjust his eyes to the darkness. It was a moonless night, but clear, without fog. He found the Lieutenant standing there at his elbow, looking off across the port bow. At first Barney could see only the dark silhouettes of the crew, busy at the big gun, and the waves tossing away into the empty gloom. Then he caught the flash of a light, off on the horizon. It glowed for only a second and disappeared. With a start he realized that the blackness where it had been was land—a low, uncertain line of shore!

"You saw it?" asked Rasch. "That was one of our men in the window of a house. Exactly one kilometer to the northward is the great Convention Hall, and beyond that the tall hotels. The signal means that the shore is not mined and no patrol boats are near. The stupid Americans trust in their blackout, but we know every target from Longport to the Inlet. Presently you will see that blackout lighted by a thousand flames."

He licked his lips as if in anticipation. "All this has been worked out according to plan," he smiled. "*My* plan! And now you will stand here and watch, while I order a little more speed to put us in perfect range."

He mounted into the conning tower and an instant later the *Sea Snake* was moving forward more swiftly, the water hissing along her sides.

The ammunition was on deck, and the gun stripped and loaded. Barney saw the giant figure of the gunner slouching beside the breech. He wondered at the docile obedience the big man had shown ever since his release from the brig. There was something wrong with him—something missing.

He moved and acted like a man walking in his sleep.

The light on land did not appear again, but the shadowy shapes of the big hotels along the beach were growing more distinct each moment as the U-boat glided nearer the shore.

Suddenly Barney stiffened. He thought he had heard a sound, very faint, coming up the coast from the south. He listened for a breathless instant until he was sure. It was the far-off, droning hum of an airplane motor.

Apparently Rasch's ears had failed to catch the sound, for at that moment he called out an order. "It's time, now, Grauner. The range is two kilometers. Take that tallest building for your first target and make every shell count!"

The big German rocked the swivel around and spun the elevating wheel with a practiced hand. Barney felt an icy coldness in his stomach as the long, wicked muzzle lowered and came to rest. Then the jarring explosion jolted against his eardrums, and a yellow flash lighted the night. Half a mile away toward shore a spout of white spray leaped up.

"You fool!" the Lieutenant's angry scream came from the conning tower. "You aimed too low! Quick—fire again!"

Grauner turned slowly away from the gun and stepped aft, past the crew, who were mechanically loading another shell. Barney saw him look up at the gesticulating young commander and heard his deep, booming laugh. Then in a flash he was over the side in a clean dive.

It was as if his action had released a trigger in the boy's brain. Without a second's hesitation he followed, snatching a deep breath as he launched his body outward through the dark. The shock of the cold sea struck him and he began swimming under water with quick, furious strokes—nursing that lungful of air—putting as much distance behind him as he could.

He kept on doggedly even when it seemed as if he must have air or die. At last his head broke the surface and he drew in a gasping breath. He had managed to kick off his sneakers during the first few seconds in the water. Now he struggled out of the heavy sweater and swam on in shirt and dungarees. A glance behind him showed the dark superstructure of the U-boat still looming close. He thought he must have traveled fifty yards in his under-water dash, but it didn't look that far. Even as he turned his head, an ugly whistling sound passed his ear and something slapped a wave a few feet beyond him. That would be Rasch—shooting with his pistol from the conning tower.

With a prayer that the Nazi's aim would still be bad on the next shot, Barney filled his lungs and dove once more.

U432

He didn't try to go so far this time. A dozen strokes, up for a breath or two, and then under again. He kept that up for minutes that seemed like hours, and at last, when his arms were weak and tired, he rolled over and floated, panting, on his back.

For the first time he had a moment to think coherently, and he tried to take stock of his situation. Why had the gunfire from the submarine stopped after Grauner's first shell? Surely there were other capable gunners in the crew. As he was lifted on the crest of a swell he looked around for his floating prison but it was nowhere in sight.

Then he remembered the plane he had heard just before plunging overboard. It must have passed above them while he was under water, and scared the Nazis into a crash dive. Where was the *Sea Snake* now, he wondered? Somewhere just under the surface, sneaking along in the dark water—perhaps right beneath him at that instant! The thought of it made him start swimming again with panicky strokes, his arms thrashing wildly. And then, sickeningly, his hand touched something more solid than yielding water.

Sheer fright paralyzed Barney for a second, and his head went under. When he came up again, choking and sputtering, ing, a hoarse voice came out of the dark, a few feet away.

"Whatsamatter, kid? Did I scare yuh?"

"Yeah," the boy gasped. "I guess—I thought it was the periscope—or a shark—or something!"

He could see Grauner's dripping head now. The big sea-man was not an easy swimmer. His arms worked constantly to keep his heavy body afloat. He acted tired.

"Which way is land?" puffed the gunner. "I can't see nothin' but waves."

Barney rubbed the water out of his eyes and looked up at the sky. There were a few stars visible. After a moment he located what looked like part of the Dipper. The North Star itself was hidden by clouds but he could see the two "pointers."

"That's north," he gestured with his arm. "An' the shore would be northwest—right over there. Let's go."

# 15

NOW that he was free of the U-boat and near a friendly coast, Barney was so elated he wanted to sing and shout. He felt as if he could swim all night, and it was a good thing he did, for his big companion was making hard work of it.

"You—go on!" Grauner panted between mouthfuls of sea. "Tell 'em—I'm comin' so they won't—be too [gulp] surprised."

"I'm in no rush," the boy answered. "Maybe I can give you a hand if you get tuckered."

At that moment a dazzling glare shot along the water, struck full in their faces, then swept on beyond them. It was a searchlight beam from a fast patrol-boat. The roar of the vessel's motors grew louder and she swept past within two hundred yards, oblivious of the swimmers.

"Too busy to mess with us, I reckon, even if she saw us," Barney said. He was going to add, "I hope she gets that *Sea Snake*," but he wasn't sure how the big German felt about it.

Grauner suddenly began to swim with all his might. "Depth charges!" he gasped. "They'll drop 'em!"

Before the boy could respond with more speed, the wind was knocked out of him as if a great fist had been driven into his middle. With numbed arms he fought feebly to stay afloat. By the time he had dragged one breath into his tortured lungs the smash of another underwater explosion hit him—then a third and a fourth. For a helpless, paralyzing moment everything went black and he lost consciousness. Then he heard a great singing in his ears and there was bright light and disturbance on the sea around him.

Half full of salt water and so weak he could barely move his hands, Barney came back to life. Above him swayed the wet side of a big motorboat and an excited American voice was yelling orders. A thrown line flicked down across his face. He clutched it with a grip of despair but when they tried to pull him up, the rope slid through his fingers. At last somebody jumped in beside him and made a hitch under his arms. And in another minute he was sprawled on the heaving after-deck of the boat.

Barney retched, gagged a few times and managed to croak out a word or two. "Another one!" he gulped. "A man—in the water." And he tried to point.

"I see him!" a voice shouted. "Just went under—right there! I'm going to dive. I can get him."

There was a thud of bare feet and a splash. The propeller churned the water slowly and the craft swung over to help with the rescue. Barney succeeded in lifting his head a little. He saw a swimmer come up, a few yards away. "Got him!" the man panted. "But the guy's big as a whale. Gimme a life-preserver!"

The white cork ring sailed overside and the sailor grabbed it. A moment later he was being pulled closer, with the limp bulk of Grauner's body dragging behind him. It took the combined efforts of the crew of five men to get the huge gunner aboard, and they worked on him in relays for several minutes before they forced the water out of his barrel chest and started him breathing. By that time Barney was on his feet and ready to lend what help he could.

When it began to look as if the rescued giant would live, the skipper turned the wheel over to one of the crew and came aft. He was a stout, middle-aged man in a soiled yacht-ing cap—one of the dozens of sportsmen boat-owners who had volunteered for auxiliary patrol duty. He might have been a prosperous lawyer or dentist in ordinary life, but tonight he was the Navy.

He eyed Barney severely and puffed out his chest and cleared his throat. "You're a German?" he asked. "*Deutscher?*"

The boy shook his head. "Nosuh," he muttered, his voice still weak and hoarse. "I'm from No'th Ca'lina."

If the captain was taken aback he tried not to show it. "Come, come," he replied gruffly. "You're wearing German sailor pants. Weren't you aboard that submarine out here?"

"Yessuh. I was a prisoner. I jumped overboard 'bout the time they fired that gun."

"Hmm. Well, we'll let the authorities get the facts. Other fellow looks like a Heinie all right. Big, ugly chap. For the present you're both under arrest. Can't put you in irons because we don't carry 'em, but we'll see you stay where you are. Mitchell, bring your rifle and keep these birds covered."

The blond sailor who had dived in after Grauner came aft grinning, with the rifle in the crook of his arm. He looked about eighteen, not much older than Barney, and he was enjoying the night's adventure as much as his captain.

"Aren't you going to take us ashore?" Barney asked the

guard, as the motorboat picked up speed and headed south-ward.

"Sure, after a while. We've got to finish our patrol first. Say, that was pretty lousy shooting. That sub o' yours was in close enough to do some real damage."

Barney jerked his thumb toward the big German, still lying prone in the cockpit. "He was the gunner," he said. "He didn't want to hit anything. Aimed low on purpose."

The offshore waters were full of craft of all kinds now. They could see cabin cruisers, like the one they were on, scurrying past in the dark, and they could hear the roaring engines of bigger boats—cutters and sub-chasers—farther out. Every few moments there would be a series of dull concussions, as more depth charges were dropped.

"You were lucky those ashcans didn't ruin you for keeps," the boy with the rifle remarked.

"Reckon they would have," said Barney, "if you hadn't spotted us. We'd swum a right smart ways, though, an' they must have been more'n a quarter mile off."

The motorboat was pitching and bobbing in choppy seas off the mouth of an inlet.

"That's Longport," said the guard. "Ocean City's just below. This is where we turn back."

The first graying of dawn was over the ocean as they passed the big Atlantic City hotels on the return trip. Off to seaward the waters were still dotted with patrol vessels, and a pair of big Navy flying boats thundered past overhead. Grauner sat up shakily and stared about him. He seemed surprised to find he was still alive.

He coughed and choked. "That you, punk?" he asked, blinking his blood-shot eyes.

"It's me, all right," Barney grinned. "Don't try to talk. I know how you feel."

The little cruiser swung over to port and bucked through the tide rip of the northern inlet. A few minutes later she was bustling past a score of similar craft toward a long dock that extended into the bay.

In the faint dawn light, Barney could make out Navy and Coast Guard uniforms and Army olive drab in the group of men waiting for them.

"Any luck?" somebody called.

The skipper had put on his brass-buttoned blue coat and was looking as important as possible.

"It's hard to say, yet awhile," he replied. "I think they must have sunk her. Anyway we picked up two survivors. Have you got a guard there? We'll want to take 'em right to Headquarters."

There was a buzz of conversation on the dock at this news. Someone snapped out an order and a pair of armed Coast Guard sailors hurried forward. The skipper went ashore first, and after him Barney and Grauner were hustled up the gang-plank. A wiry young Navy Lieutenant pushed through the staring crowd and took brisk command.

"Clear the dock," he ordered. "Put them in my car, men. Captain, have you a mate you can leave in charge of your boat? Good. I'll want you to come with me."

They were whisked through the streets at high speed, the Lieutenant's peremptory horn clearing a path for them at traffic intersections. In a few minutes they pulled up before a hotel entrance and the guards marched them inside before passers-by knew what was happening. For the first time in his life Barney found himself in an elevator. He was almost as much frightened by that swift ascent as he had been at any time since his capture at Caldee.

They waited briefly in an anteroom while the Lieutenant made his report. Then they were ushered into a big, pleasant room where electric lights were still on behind the blackout curtains. Four men sat there around a table littered with papers and empty coffee cups. They looked grim and tired but very much awake. One was a Navy three-striper, one a Coast Guard Lieutenant Commander. The other two were in Army Air Force uniforms. The senior officer present had the single star of a Brigadier General and the young man beside him wore a First Lieutenant's silver bars.

The motorboat captain was called forward first. Somewhat abashed by so much gold braid, he told his story haltingly but in fairly accurate detail.

"All right," the General nodded when he had asked a question or two. "Now we'll have the prisoners. The young fellow first. Commander, you speak German. Will you interpret for him?"

"Don't need to talk German," said Barney calmly. "I'm an American."

The General frowned. "Very well," he said. "Speak up. You were on a German submarine, weren't you?"

The boy explained once more that he was a prisoner. Then he tried to outline his story from the start. It was hard going because of frequent interruptions and the quite evident disbelief on the faces of the men in front of him.

Unexpectedly, Grauner's deep voice rumbled through the room. "The kid is telling the truth," he growled. "A spy, name of Ohlgren, brought him aboard off Hatteras, like he says."

"Quiet, please," snapped the Commander. "We'll hear from you later. General, I don't see much use in going further with this boy. We'll check on his yarn, of course, but meanwhile I suggest we lock him up."

"Wait, sir," said Barney in desperation. "If I could send word to Slug Martin, he'd clear the whole thing up. He's a pilot down at Kitty Hawk—"

The Air Force Lieutenant had been sprawling in his chair. Now he sat suddenly erect. "Who's that again, youngster?" he drawled. "Slug Martin, did you say? Well, bust mah cacky britches!"

He turned to the Brigadier. "Will you let me send a message, General, suh?" he asked. "Slug Martin roomed with me at Randolph Field. He's a sho'-nuff Longhorn an' straight as they come."

The General nodded. "No harm in that," he replied. "Go ahead."

The Lieutenant grinned at Barney. "Listen, son," he said. "You got some kind o' pass-word would let Slug know it was you?"

The boy thought a minute. "Caldee Castle," he answered. "He knew I was headed there that night."

"C-A-L-D-E-E." The airman was jotting the letters on a sheet of paper. Then he rose and sauntered toward the door. "Keep your chin up," he whispered as he passed Barney.

"All right," the General nodded toward Grauner. "You seem to speak English too, though with a different accent. I suppose you're another kidnapping case. What's your story?"

The ex-wrestler caught the irony in the officer's words and shook his bull-like head. "No," he boomed. "I am a German subject—an enemy. I have been a gunner on the U-boats since the war began and I have sent many of your ships to the bottom. But I am no Nazi. That is why I disobeyed that young pig's order, and why I went overboard last night. You can do what you like with me. But if you do not believe the boy's story you are fools."

He spoke slowly and heavily, without a trace of his usual slang. When he finished there was silence in the room, broken only by the tapping of the General's pencil on the table.

At length the gray-mustached officer nodded. "You'll be held under guard," he said. "There'll be some further questioning and you'll be given a fair chance to prove whether you should be treated as a prisoner of war. If you were attempting to land as a spy, that's another matter, and you know the consequences, of course."

Grauner made a short, stiff bow.

The General turned to the Commander, and he in turn addressed the young Lieutenant who had brought them from the dock. "Take charge of your prisoners," he said. "Better put them in Room 15 for the time being. And it seems to be breakfast time. You might want to give them something to eat."

Early morning sun was streaming in the windows of the outer room when they passed through. Barney stared and blinked at the golden rays. He suddenly realized it was the first sunshine he had seen since he left the Carolina beach!

They were taken to a bare-walled room with barred windows. Half a dozen chairs and a small table made up all the furniture, but it was far more comfortable than a jail cell. They were told to sit down and the two guards took chairs near the door, watching their prisoners warily.

Barney felt very tired, now that he had a chance to rest. The nausea that had bothered him after he was pulled out of the sea was gone at last, but he had a dull sort of headache. The idea of food held no interest for him.

Yet a few minutes later, when the door was opened to

admit an Army messman carrying a tray, he found he was all at once ravenously hungry. There were two plates of ham and eggs, bread with real butter, and cups of steaming fragrant coffee. The tray was put down on the table. One of the Coast Guard sailors glowered at Barney and the German.

"Well," he said, "it's for you. Whatcha waitin' for. Come an' get it!"

Grauner chuckled as he pulled up his chair. "I kind of remembered grub like this in America," he said. "But then I thought I must be kiddin' myself. Punk, you've really got a country here!"

Before they had finished their meal the guard was changed, and a couple of rangy lads in khaki replaced the sailors. One of the newcomers eyed Barney with interest. "Tell me yo're from No'th Ca'lina," he remarked. "Ev' been to Raleigh?"

Barney grinned to hear the true tarheel twang in the soldier's voice. "No," he said. "I'm tidewater, myself. We-all travel up Norfolk-way when we get a yen for city sights. Hear it's right pretty country, though, 'round Raleigh," he added for politeness.

"Shucks," the young guard replied with conviction. "If yo're a Heinie ah'll eat a mule, plow, harness an' all!"

It was a few minutes after the empty dishes were cleared away that a sharp rap came at the door. The man who entered was the big Texas Lieutenant who had volunteered to send Slug Martin a message. He smiled from ear to ear.

"Got good news fo' you, son," he announced. "The ol' rattlesnake's on his way right now. I talked to him on the phone an' he's got a special leave to fly up an' take a look at you!"

"Gee!" Barney cried. "That's swell! How long you reckon it'll take him? That old crate he flies isn't so fast."

"Maybe it wasn't, last time you saw him," the Lieutenant laughed. "But he's got a P-38 now, an' he'll sho'-nuff give her the spurs. If he don't stop any place to powder his nose I'd expect him along in two hours."

# 16

THERE was no clock in the guarded room. Barney tried to pass the time by thinking about other things—his father and mother—little Anna—Judy, the pony—the *Jennie May*. He'd have to get the news to them at home some way. Maybe Slug would lend him money to telegraph. Then his thoughts came back to that two-tailed streak of P-38 Lightning, winging north.

He got up and walked to the window and back. "What time is it now?" he asked the North Carolina soldier.

"Nine-thirty. It's only an hour an' a half since the Lieutenant was in here. Keep yo' shirt on, son."

But Barney didn't hear him. He was racing to the window again.

Far off in the sky he had heard the high-pitched whine of motors, and now, as he looked upward, he caught the glint of sun on an aluminum speck coming from the southwest. The plane circled, losing speed and altitude. He could see it clearly at last—the unmistakable twin-sparred outline of a P-38.

"It's Slug!" yelled Barney. "He's coming down now—headed for the field!"

The next quarter hour of waiting was the hardest. The boy began to wonder if he'd been wrong. There were plenty of Lightnings along the coast. Maybe this was a different one. And yet—streaking in so high from the southwest—he couldn't be mistaken.

A tread of boots came swiftly along the corridor and there were voices—and a peal of Texas laughter that sounded like the neigh of a horse. It was Slug, all right—Slug with his long frame swathed in heavy flying togs—his goggles pushed up on his helmet. He stood there, arms akimbo, and squinted at Barney with a stern, judicial air.

"Don't look much like the feller I knew," he announced. "Ol' Barney Cannon always had a nice brown coat o' tan. This boy's sort o' pindlin'—pale an' wan. Mean-lookin' cuss, too. Reckon we'd better leave him in durance vile."

"Aw, gee, Slug!" Barney pleaded. "Quit fooling an' say you're glad to see me!"

Martin's friend was red-faced with mirth, but Slug didn't laugh. He strode forward and seized the boy's shoulders with both hands. "Darn right I am!" he said soberly. "I came as quick as I could, but before I left I sent a jeep down the road with a message to your folks. Wish I could see your ma's face when she heard!"

He turned to the other airman. "Come on," he said, "let's get him out o' here. This ol' horned toad," he explained to Barney, "is Lieutenant Sam Breen."

After the introduction, Barney looked at Grauner. The big man's scarred and ugly face was almost gentle at that moment. "So long, punk," he growled.

"I'll tell 'em the truth about you," said the boy, "an' they'll believe me, now. An' if there's anything I can do—while you're in prison camp—let me know."

He put out his hand. The gunner squeezed it in his own vast paw and grinned understandingly. "*Auf Wiedersehen*," he chuckled. "You knew the German talk all the time, didn't you? Well, I never gave you away."

Once outside the room, the two fliers took Barney directly to the Headquarters office where he had been questioned earlier. The General accepted Slug's identification of the boy and signed a paper that set him free. "I'd like you to stay in town for a day or two," he said as they shook hands. "There may be some further information you can give us—about that island base in the Bahamas."

"Yes, sir," said Barney. "I'd like to, sir."

"And by the way, Lieutenant, do you know whether that enemy agent, Ohlgren, has been taken in custody? Not yet, eh? Well, I'll start something on that at once. Report back to me tomorrow and bring the boy with you."

Slug and his fellow pilot saluted and they took their departure. Lieutenant Breen was still on duty. "Got to leave you now," he said, "but I'll see you tonight an' we'll make up for lost time."

Going down in the elevator the lanky Texan cast a quizzical eye over Barney's costume. It was the same one in which he had been fished out of the ocean. "Seems to me," said Slug, "that a shirt an' a pair o' Heinie britches are a mite sketchy for the Atlantic City boardwalk. Soon as I change to light uniform, I reckon our first job is to get some decent, respectable clothes on you."

Barney's protests were in vain. The flier announced that he had cleaned out the officers' room in a poker game the night before, and the money was burning holes in his pocket. They went into a ready-to-wear store and outfitted him with underwear, socks, shirts, a pair of gray flannel trousers, a tan sweater and saddle shoes. With his hair combed he looked like a new man.

"Look, Slug," he told his friend when they were outside again. "I found this in the pocket o' those old pants I had on. I'd forgotten about it, but maybe it's something pretty important."

What he held in his hand was a tightly rolled piece of oilskin with something hard inside. "I reckon it's spoiled by now—where it's been was plenty wet. But I'll tell you about it an' see what you think."

They found a bench under a kind of summerhouse on the seaward side of the boardwalk, and Barney took up the tale of his adventures from the beginning. When he told how Kramer, at Caldee, had suggested disposing of his boat, Slug's face hardened.

"The low-down skunk!" he said. "He worked out a slicker plan than that, even—one that had me fooled. When you weren't home that mornin', your dad was pretty upset, an' started out in the *Jennie May* lookin' for you. He got up as far as Manteo an' found your boat tied to one o' the piers. He went ashore an' the first feller he saw was a young loafer sittin' in front o' the store. Sure, he'd seen you, he said.

You'd come up there the night before an' drunk a coke with him an' told him you were runnin' away—goin' to join the Navy. I always did suspect that yarn, but your dad let on he believed it. Anyhow he kept waitin' for a letter from you. Your ma was mighty anxious, too, but I reckon young Anna was the hardest hit of all. She didn't say much but she wouldn't eat an' her eyes looked like burnt holes in a blanket.

"I stirred up my skipper to tackle Intelligence again, an' they went down to Caldee an' really searched the place. Couldn't find anything out o' the way, so I decided you really had run off to the Navy. They've kept an eye on that Ohlgren gang ever since. It won't take long to round 'em up now."

Barney went on with his yarn, describing Captain Von Sturm and Rasch and the first hours aboard the submarine.

"One thing I noticed right soon," he told his friend, "was the way those Diesels kept on running while we were under water."

"You mean they didn't cut over to the batteries when they dove?"

"Didn't even have any batteries that I ever found. They had extra torpedoes stored under the crew room where the batteries ought to have been."

The Texan whistled. "I did hear something like that," he said. "Some U-boat the British captured. No batteries aboard, an' the engines were supposed to run on a mixture of gases—hydrogen an' oxygen, I think it was—long as they were below the surface."

Barney started forward, his eyes wide. "Sa-a-ay!" he breathed. "Hydrogen an' oxygen—"

"Why? What about it?" asked Slug.

"Nothing. Only—well, I'll tell you the rest o' the story."

He mentioned the hint, let fall by one of the German sailors, that the submarine could get along without oil. And he told about his discovery of the big evaporators, and the feed pipes running to the engines. When he came to the night and day spent at Hangman's Cay, he went into detail about the can of chemicals that Hans had spilled, and the engineer's remarks as they scooped it up.

"If the water didn't get in an' spoil it, I've got some o' the stuff here," he said. And with care he unwrapped the oilskin cover of the match-safe. There was a stain of salt and rust on a part of the little metal container. But when he removed the tight-fitting cap and looked in, the gray-brown powder seemed to be dry.

"By gumption!" he cried. "I b'lieve it's still all right!"

They sniffed at the material cautiously and Slug poured a few grains into his palm. "I never got very far in chemistry at school," he said, "an' I wouldn't have even a sneakin' idea what this is. But I reckon there's some hot-shot chemists in Washin'ton that could find out pronto. Hydrogen an' oxygen—from $H_2O$? Why not? Most likely it's the Navy that ought to have this information, but the Navy an' Air Force seem to work pretty close together here. Show it to the General in the mornin'."

The rest of Barney's narrative went quickly, for the experience of the night before was still too fresh in his mind for him to relish talking about it. However, he went to some pains to explain Grauner's position. "He's a German—no question o' that," he admitted. "An' he was a good sailor under the old captain. But he hated Rasch an' his Nazi stooges. It was disobeying orders when he was told to shoot that poor guy in the water that got him thrown in the brig. I reckon they'll hold it against him that he can talk English so well, but shucks! he's no more a spy than I am!"

The town was full of soldiers, many of them wearing Air Force insignia. They marched past by companies and platoons, going to classroom or to drill. The submarine commander's information had been accurate, for the big hotels were completely occupied by the Army.

"Reckon you wouldn't get much kick out of a swim," Slug grinned. "S'pose we have some lunch an' take in a movie."

That evening they went to Lieutenant Breen's quarters and Barney listened with delight while the two Texans kidded each other and swapped cowboy and aviation yarns. But he had spent a fairly busy twenty-four hours. Around nine o'clock he dropped off to sleep in the middle of one of Slug's tallest stories.

When he woke there was morning sun coming in the windows and he was lying on a cot in the bedroom at the Air Force officers' quarters. From the next room came the smell of coffee and the cheerful clatter of dishes. Barney had the luxury of a shower before he dressed in his new clothes and went in to breakfast. Slug Martin, Sam Breen and a couple of other Army pilots were around the table.

"A good thing you finally woke up, son," said Breen. "Pull up an' eat hearty. We've got a date over at Headquarters in half an hour."

It was an impressive array of gold braid that they found in the General's room. The Brigadier himself was flanked by two Colonels, and a Captain from Naval Intelligence in

Washington had joined the two blue-uniformed officers. Breen and Martin, with Barney, were ushered in without delay, and the boy was somewhat embarrassed to find himself the center of attention.

For the benefit of the Navy four-striper he was asked to tell the story of his capture once more. The Captain shot a few searching questions at him and finally nodded. "I've heard of Von Sturm," he said. "A first-class sailor out of the old German navy. Wish I'd known he was ashore. I'd have enjoyed taking him prisoner myself and spinning a yarn or two with him. I expect I've fought him more than once back in 'seventeen and 'eighteen. Well, we caught Ohlgren and his crew at home yesterday. Got 'em all where they belong. Now, young man, I'd like to hear what you can tell us about that U-boat you were on."

Barney began once more. "She was the U-432. One of the Cobra squadron, with an ugly-looking snake painted on her conning tower."

The Navy Captain's lips tightened and he nodded again. "I've seen 'em," he said briefly.

The boy continued, giving a very fair description of the *Sea Snake's* hull plan and armament. "There were some queer things about her though, different from most subs." He hesitated, looked at Slug and went on.

"For one thing, she didn't have any batteries, except maybe little ones aft. An' I don't think she burned oil in her Diesels."

Every one of the officers was leaning forward intently, staring at him.

"That sounds sort o' crazy, but she had tremendous big evaporators right forward o' the engine room, an' for a long time I couldn't figure why she needed so much fresh water. Then one day I saw the Chief Engineer pouring some kind o' powder into a contraption that must have done something to the water. Maybe Grauner could tell you more about it if he'd talk. But anyhow, I got hold of a little o' that powder —an' here it is."

He laid the match-safe on the long table and drew a deep breath.

The General took off the metal cap, peered inside and passed the little container along to the Captain, who handled it as if it had been a diamond necklace. After a moment's examination, the Naval Intelligence officer replaced the cover with care. "I'd like to take this down by plane this afternoon," he told the others. "There's enough here for an analysis. We've suspected something like this for months, but we figured they were doing it by electrolysis. Getting hold of some of their chemical—dry—is a piece of extraordinary luck. I congratulate you, young man!"

Barney flushed and looked down at his feet in their new shoes. But his ordeal wasn't over yet.

"Let's hear something about that island base where the U-boat put in," said the Captain briskly. He spread a big-scale chart of the Bahama archipelago on the table. "About where would you place it?"

Barney bent above the map for several minutes. Many of the small islands were named, but there was no sign of one called Hangman's Cay.

"It could be 'most anywhere along here, sir," he replied, pointing to an area of some fifty by a hundred miles, to the east of the main group of islands. "It's small, and I never got a good look at it in daylight, but I covered it pretty well in the dark. I'd know it if I saw it again."

"Ah," the General murmured. "That brings us to the point, doesn't it, Captain? You see, Cannon, we have a little plan to locate that island. I've no doubt you're anxious to get home and see your family. We'll try not to postpone it too long. But first there's a rather important job to be done."

His eyes turned toward Slug Martin. "Lieutenant, I've

had your commanding officer on the wire. He's extended your leave for special duty, and your pursuit plane will be flown back to Kitty Hawk tomorrow. This morning there's a DC-3 starting south at eleven-thirty, and there'll be seats aboard for you and young Cannon. I want you to report to Colonel Brighton, at Miami, for further orders. Your trip is entirely confidential, of course. Meanwhile, you both may be glad to hear that the man Grauner will be treated as a prisoner of war."

Barney was still in a daze when they reached the corridor outside. "Gosh, Slug, what did he mean about the plane south?" he asked his friend.

"You an' I are goin' to do some fancy travelin'," the Texan laughed. "An', boy, we ought to see action before it's over!"

# 17

SLUG MARTIN packed his bag in a hurry, and he and Barney found an Army jeep waiting for them at the curb. There was an attractive young WAAC behind the wheel.

"Good morning, Lieutenant," she saluted. "Are you the two important passengers I'm to take to the airfield?"

"Important is right, soldier," the Texan grinned. "Can you handle this rubber-tired bronc, or do you want me to drive?"

"I think I can manage very well," she replied with a smile. "It's been my job for three months."

She drove the fast little car with an expert skill that left Barney breathless and admiring. Even Slug was respectful when she whirled into the airport a few minutes later. "Ma'am," he said, "my apologies. You can do my drivin' any time. An' I'd be plumb happy to know how they call you."

"Eleven twenty-five," she announced, with a glance at her wrist-watch. "There's your plane, warming up on the line. It's been a pleasure, Lieutenant," she added with a twinkle. "The name is Clifton, Mary B., Auxiliary First Class, Headquarters Company."

They found most of the seats in the transport plane already occupied by officers of the various Services, but there were two places reserved for them toward the rear. They sat down behind a pair of Navy men.

It was Barney's first air trip of any length and he meant to savor its thrills to the full. Hardly had he settled himself by the window when the transport rumbled down the strip, picked up speed and took off so smoothly that he never knew when the wheels left the ground. In another moment there were sand and pines and houses flitting past below him. With less commotion than the *Jennie May* made, leaving the home dock, they were on their way.

Slug was talking to a Navy Lieutenant in the seat in front of him. "Hear you been havin' a little excitement," he commented. "What's the dope? Did you get that Heinie?"

"Not officially," the two-striper answered. "But if he got away from that pattern of ash-cans we dropped off the

*Shinnebago*, it's a miracle. There were a couple of oil-slicks out there in the morning. That's all we know about it."

Barney said nothing but he wondered. He knew the toughness of the *Sea Snake's* hide, and the speed with which she could hunt safety on the bottom. It was hard to think of all those people he had lived with as possible corpses. The rough-tongued bosun and the treacherous Froelich, the barrel-bellied cook and young Hans, stupid but harmless.

Far beneath the plane a broad stretch of water opened, and the boy saw dots of ships—a tanker and a rusty tramp steamer and fishing-boats and two grim, gray destroyers. That was Delaware Bay, he thought. Ten minutes later they were over land again, farms and villages reaching southward as far as the eye could see. Delaware, then Maryland, and the long spike of the Cape Charles Peninsula, where blue water sparkled in the distance to left and right.

A little after one the plane roared across Hampton Roads and banked in a long spiral for the landing at Norfolk. Barney caught only glimpses of the city and the huge naval installations but he had an excited sense of being home again—close to the land and water he knew so well.

With Slug he hurried over to the airport buildings and ate lunch while the plane refueled. Four or five of the Navy men had left at Norfolk but others appeared to take their places. In twenty minutes they were aloft again.

"You reckon we'll fly over Kitty Hawk an'—an' home?" Barney asked hopefully. But Slug thought not.

"We'll be hittin' a bee-line for Florida now," he answered. "Nearest place you're likely to see is Edenton, an' we won't be back over the coast again much before Charleston."

So the boy had to content himself with a quick look at Albemarle Sound and the Pamlico River. After that the long trip seemed to drag. They made their next landing at Savannah in midafternoon, and at six-thirty the plane rolled down the long runway of the Miami airport.

A shower had just ended and the sun, breaking through the clouds, glistened on green palmettos and white buildings.

"End o' the line—all change," Slug announced. "We'd better get us a meal first an' then report to Colonel Brighton. He'll be expectin' us this evenin'."

They found the Colonel and his aides waiting for them at Bomber Command Headquarters. He was a lean, leathery-faced airman with steel-gray eyes and a crisp, short manner of speech.

"Lieutenant Martin—Mr. Cannon," he said, returning Slug's salute, "sit down. Let's get to business."

He picked up a sheaf of papers. "The General has given me the gist of your report, Cannon. Our job is to find that base. We've had patrols over those waters a dozen times in the last two weeks and haven't seen a periscope. So it's a bit tough for us to believe there's anything there. But we'll take your word. Did you see enough of the island to give me a rough idea of its shape and size?"

Barney took the pencil and paper he offered and thought a minute. "I'd say the outside reef ran pretty much in a circle," he said. "A couple o' breaks in it, like this. One on the northeast side where the U-boat went through."

He continued sketching in the outline, then paused again. "The island's almost round, too. There's a little cove right about here, an' a long old fish-pier built out beside it. The shack at the land end is all falling to pieces. Looks as if no-body'd been there for years. But they've dug out a berth alongside for a submarine an' got it covered over with a net so you couldn't see it from overhead. Up this way there's a canteen an' maybe some other buildings. An' over here, close to the shore," he indicated with his pencil, "there's a long stone house under the palm trees. No windows in it, so I figured it might be a storage place for torpedoes an' shells an' such.

"That's about all I can tell you," he concluded. "The island itself can't be more'n about half a mile across. Wish I could give you latitude an' longitude, but it would be a plain guess."

Colonel Brighton bent above the sketch with a thoughtful frown. "I couldn't swear I haven't looked down on such an island," he said. "Has sort of a familiar look. But there are hundreds like it, of course. What do you say, Captain?"

He passed the paper to the officer beside him.

"We generally do our scouting at three or four thousand feet," the Captain replied. "The pier and the shack would look harmless enough at that altitude. Maybe we'd have better luck at low level, sir."

"Right. Your plane ready?"

"Ready any time, sir. Crew's standing by."

"Well, you won't start before morning but it may be early. I've got to wait for word from the Navy. They're putting a couple of destroyers on this job, but one of 'em needed twelve hours to be ready for sea.

"Here's our plan. First, Captain Owens, meet Lieutenant Martin and"—he glanced at his notes—"Barney Cannon. Martin, ever flown a four-motored ship?"

"I've had five or six hours in a Fortress, sir."

"This one's a Liberator, but never mind that. You'll go as co-pilot. And you, Cannon—there'll be room for you in the nose, with the bombardier. I want you where you can spot that island if possible. Captain Owens will find you quarters tonight and I'd advise you both to get a good night's sleep."

*　　*　　*

Barney was too excited to do as much sleeping as the Colonel would have wished. Captain Owens took them to one of the big Miami Beach hotels which had been taken over by the Air Force. As guests they were given a double room and bath, with windows that looked out on the starlit sea. Long after the rangy Texan in the other bed was peacefully snoring, the boy lay there listening to the murmur of surf along the sand. So much had happened since morning, and so much might happen tomorrow, that his mind was in a whirl.

Finally he dozed off and slept soundly till daylight. Slug was already up and singing in the shower. They were both full of high spirits and anticipation. But before breakfast the Captain came in with a long face.

"Looks as if we'd be hung up another day," he announced. "The Navy boys are doing their best, but that destroyer was in a fight last week and it's taking a little longer to put her in shape than they figured. Something about the firing mechanism on her forward battery. They're flying some new parts in from Norfolk. Come on down to breakfast and meet some of the gang you'll fly with in the *Chattanooga Choo-Choo.*"

The regular co-pilot, the bombardier and the navigator of the big bomber were all at table in the officers' mess and they rose, grinning, to be introduced to Slug and Barney. All three were Second Lieutenants. The bombardier was a big, slow-spoken Iowan, called Windy by his pals. Eddie, the navigator, was a studious-looking youngster from Massachusetts. And the poker-faced co-pilot, known as Stoney, was from Tennessee. It was he, they said, who had christened their ship.

Windy made a place at the table beside him for Barney. "Hear you're goin' to ride with me," he smiled. "You'll like it out there in the greenhouse. If there's anything to see at all, you can see it from there."

"Do you expect to be carrying any bombs?" the boy asked.

"Oh, sure. All our patrol trips we do. Generally we're loaded with depth bombs. They do a mighty pretty job on a sub. This trip we'll have regular five-hundred-pounders."

"Gee! Have you bombed many U-boats?"

"A couple we're sure of. Maybe one or two others that we didn't hit square."

After breakfast they went out to the field, where the *Chattanooga Choo-Choo* was getting a thorough going-over inside the big hangar. She looked enormous to Barney when he stood under her wing—two or three times as large as the transport in which he had come south. The crew men were checking her four great radial motors under the eagle eye of the crew chief. He was a lanky, tobacco-chewing Maine man known as Elmer—one of those born mechanics worth their weight in gold to the Air Force.

"She'll do, Jack," he told Captain Owens. Officers and non-coms all seemed to be on first-name terms in this bomber team. "You c'n take her to Africa this minute, 'f you want to."

The Captain chuckled. "Won't be that far, this trip, but I like to have plenty of gas on any mission."

Other men came up and were introduced. Nate, the radio operator, was a stocky Jewish boy from Brooklyn. And the two gunners, who manned the tail and top turrets, hailed from Arizona and Alaska. Barney never got their names, but they were alike in being on the small side—tough, wiry, keen-eyed men with fighting faces.

Other bomber-crews, in flight togs, passed on their way to the big planes. The bombardiers carried their bombsights in canvas covers like fat suitcases. There was some good-natured ribbing.

"What's the matter, Jack?" one pilot yelled. "I didn't think they'd ground you just for bein' a punk bridge player!"

"Gwan!" somebody else replied. "It's woman-trouble! Windy danced twice with Miss Miami Beach last night. Didn't you hear?"

The other bombers took off on their missions and a pair of huge gasoline trucks rolled up to the hangar. Hoses were unreeled and thousands of gallons of high-octane fuel were pumped into the Liberator's wing tanks. Barney walked back under the long fuselage, staring fascinated at the twin rudders and the gunner's turret in the tail, with its vicious-looking pair of 50 mm. guns. It was hard to imagine that giant machine, bigger than a locomotive, winging through the thin air miles above the earth.

After an hour or two they went back to the officers' quarters and pored over charts of the Eastern Caribbean until lunchtime. There were at least a dozen unnamed dots of reef and island scattered over two or three degrees of latitude in the general area Barney indicated. Eddie, the navigator, was absorbed by the problem. He plotted a course that would take them east by south to the neighborhood of Watling Island and allow them to zigzag northwestward over every unidentified reef and cay.

"That looks pretty good," Jack Owens commented. "What would you say—about five hours, all told?"

"Not more than that. Nearer four, I'd make it. Where are we supposed to pick up those destroyers?"

"If that repair job is done tonight they'll get off around three in the morning and steam up through Providence Channel. That'll put 'em somewhere north of Eleuthera Island by ten. We'll keep radio contact so they can move in fast if we spot anything."

That afternoon Slug and Barney went for a swim in the warm surf. They were coming up the beach, full of sun and high spirits, when Windy, the bombardier, ran out to meet them. "Jack just got a call from the Commander," he grinned. "Ol' destroyer's all fixed up, an' the mission's on for tomorrow. We're due to take off early—seven o'clock on the nose!"

# 18

SIX-FORTY-FIVE by Slug's watch when they reached the airport, and the crew was there before them. Another fair day—one of those rare Florida mornings when the air was cool and clear as crystal. The early sun slanted across the vast field, and the shadow of the bomber stretched away for half a mile. Seeing her outside in the sunlight he saw that she was painted in two colors—greenish brown on top and sides—gray-blue along her belly. That made sense, he thought. The huge plane would be hard to see from far below, blending with the sky.

Slug climbed up into the pilot's compartment with Captain Jack Owens and they checked over the instruments together. Elmer was prowling around his beloved engines, checking them after their warm-up. The ground crew loaded the bombs from wheeled dollies and the bomb bay doors were closed. Accompanied by an armed guard, Windy brought his bombsight out from the safe and clambered into the glass nose.

Then the gunners came from the hangar, loaded with long belts of ammunition that trailed like wreaths from their shoulders. Eddie, the navigator, laid out his charts and instruments on his little work table inside the plane. And Nate fiddled expertly with the dials of the radio transmitter.

Barney had been outfitted with a sheep-lined coat and warm, loose trousers to go over his regular clothes. In addition he wore a parachute. At the bombardier's invitation he crawled out into the nose and took the right-hand seat, at Windy's side.

"Clear one," the pilot called, and Elmer shouted back, "Clear!"

The number one engine turned its propeller over, coughed and began a steady roar. Number two picked up the rhythm, then three and four.

Windy handed Barney a pair of earphones and a microphone and put on his own. With the motors going, all communication in the plane would be by interphone. They heard Owens call Operations and get his field clearance, and in a moment the giant bomber was rumbling down the runway, picking up speed second by second.

"Wheels off at 659.52," came the pilot's voice. "Got it, Eddie?"

"659.52. Roger," Eddie answered.

They were well above the trees and shooting straight into the morning sun. Ahead the sea glittered like a million little mirrors. The plane climbed steadily.

"How high are we now?" Barney asked, thinking he was speaking to Windy. The answer came back in Slug Martin's voice.

"Twenty-two hundred," the Texan announced. "An' back where I come from boys are seen an' not heard."

"Who let that guy in?" came another voice—Eddie's, he thought. "I ask you—who's the most important man on this mission? Barney Cannon. Let him talk if he likes."

Windy grinned and slapped Barney's knee. He had already placed the Norden bombsight in position. The boy looked at it with awe, knowing how carefully it was protected from spying eyes. He covered the microphone with his hand and leaned over to yell in Windy's ear.

"You reckon it's okay for me to see that thing?" he pointed.

The bombardier nodded. "Colonel ordered you should

ride out here, didn't he? Well, that makes everything jake."

Barney bent over to look back under the wing. The land was already behind them, out of his line of vision. Yet the great plane scarcely seemed to be moving. He risked another question—into the mike, this time. "How fast are we going?"

"Hitting about two-seventy-five. That's loafing speed for the ol' *Choo-Choo*." It was Windy who answered, right beside him, and he was pointing to the air speed indicator on the small instrument panel in the nose. Barney was ashamed of himself. He should have noticed the dials sooner. A look at the altimeter told him they had climbed now to three thousand feet.

The Captain's voice came over the interphone. "Time to give those destroyers a buzz, Nate. They ought to be well out toward their station by now."

After a moment there was a faint sound of rapid-fire dots and dashes, repeated several times. The answer came back soon, and at the end of five minutes or so the radioman had decoded it.

"They're right on schedule, Jack," he announced. "Everything going fine."

The bomber passed Bimini, a speck in the ocean on their left, and twenty minutes later they sighted the big island of

Andros ahead.

"After we cross that northern point," Windy told the boy, "it won't be long before we pass Nassau. Keep your eye peeled. Might see the Windsors out for a stroll."

But they got only a glimpse of the Bahamian capital, miles to the northward.

Soon the sea seemed to be full of little islands—palm-fringed, reef-circled cays, reaching away to the horizon like a string of beads. Some of them looked just the size and shape of Hangman's Cay, though Barney knew the island they were hunting must be hundreds of miles away.

At eight-twenty Captain Owens checked with the navigator. "Where would you put us now, Eddie?"

"I haven't peeked out for a while, Jack, but if you can't see Watling Island down there at one-twenty degrees, there's a twist in my slide rule."

Barney heard Owens chuckle and his eyes followed Windy's pointing finger to a dark mass on the horizon, off what he would have called the starboard bow.

"Here we go then, on the new course," the pilot announced, and the Liberator's wings banked gracefully as she swung her nose to the left. They cruised northeastward for ten minutes, then zigzagged to the northwest. Gradually they had lost altitude until now they were skimming along, a thousand feet above the water. As the sun rose higher it grew warm there in the glassed-in nose of the plane. Barney felt himself getting drowsy, staring down at the monotonous procession of waves. He stripped off his heavy coat and tried hard to keep awake.

"Everybody on the alert," barked Jack Owens. "From here on we could sight that sub base any minute now."

That warning shook the boy out of his sleepiness. He searched the horizon constantly, ahead and on both sides, for glimpses of land. Several times in the next half hour he thought he had found something. But the distant islands, as they approached, turned out to be too large, or the wrong shape, or little rocks completely bare of trees. Then they swung eastward again and for fifty miles not even a coral reef broke the placid blue expanse.

"Sure got fine visibility today," Windy remarked. "If there's anything to see, we ought to see it."

Occasionally they sighted a small coasting schooner or a sponge-fisherman's boat, and once they flew over a deep-laden freighter, plowing along without escort. Painted big on her sides was the neutral flag of Portugal. Eddie gave Nate her position and the radioman reported it back to their base in Miami as a matter of routine. Then they were over empty ocean once more.

"Ho hum! Time to change course again," the Captain said. Answering her rudders and ailerons the big ship banked over for the turn. And at that instant Barney sprang half out of his seat and let out a yell.

"Wait! There's some kind o' land over there to starboard!"

The *Chattanooga Choo-Choo* lurched back on her course, and Slug Martin's low whistle came over the interphone. "He's right, Cap'n. Thar she blows! How about goin' over to have a look-see?"

Somehow Barney knew that this was Hangman's Cay. He knew it by a prickly feeling in his scalp while the island was still a fuzzy blur of palms half a dozen miles away. And he knew it more surely every second as the outline of the reef and the shore came into view.

They were almost over it when Windy spoke. "Looks like another blank. Nobody home there."

"No!" cried Barney. "It's the island! Look there—see the old dock and the little shack? Those trees alongside the dock are fakes—just netting and palm leaves."

"You're sure, are you?" the pilot's voice came sharply. "Those buildings must be well hidden. Okay, take a quick sight, Eddie, and get the position. We won't turn back, or act as if we'd seen anything."

"Want me to tell the destroyers, Jack?" the radioman asked.

"No. Not yet. Those Jerries might get suspicious if they heard us start to use the radio. I'll tell you when."

Barney stared back as long as he could see the island. But there was no sign of life—no movement except the waving of palm fronds in the breeze.

When they were ten miles away and beyond the vision of anyone on the cay, Owens swung northwestward and began to climb. "All right," he said. "We can talk to the Navy now. Give 'em the exact bearings and tell 'em we'll meet 'em on their way down."

In a few minutes, Nate reported back. "They've started, Skipper. Steaming full speed, and expect to be off the island by fourteen-thirty. You goin' to stick around an' see the fun?"

"Could be. We've got fuel enough. While we're at it we may as well keep an eye out for stray U-boats."

Sighting the island had driven all the sleepiness out of Barney's system. He was keyed up now, and tense. It was hard to sit still.

The Liberator droned along at three thousand feet, with her engines throttled down to save gas. Windy was speculating on his chances of using the "eggs" in his bomb bay.

"Wonder if they've got any antiaircraft on that island," he said. "I'd like to try some low-level stuff if we can get in."

"I only saw the place at night, an' I didn't bump into any guns," the boy told him. "But I reckon they're prepared for 'most anything. They don't do things half-way. Say—look, Windy. What's that little whitish streak over yonder?"

"Golly-Peter!" the bombardier ejaculated. "Periscope wake or I'm a wall-eye mule! Got it, Jack? Fifty degrees. She's divin'! Let's go!"

"Might be one of ours," the pilot answered. "Get a quick check, Eddie. We don't want to lose her."

There was a hurried jumble of dot-dash code, a dragging wait of half a minute, and then the answer came back. "No U. S. submarines in this area. Give her the works!"

Owens had been circling and losing altitude to keep the diving U-boat in view. She was completely submerged, but the tell-tale streak of foam still showed on the surface as the big plane straightened out for her bombing run.

Windy was in full command now. "Little more left rudder," he snapped. "Right! Hold her as she is!"

His big fingers manipulated the bombsight dials quickly and surely. The bomb bay doors were open. "Coming on the target!" he called, and his left hand was steady on the bomb-release lever.

"Bombs away!" he yelled. Leaning far over, Barney could see the two five-hundred-pounders hurtling down, keeping pace at first with the plane, then dipping their noses straight toward the shadow, just below the surface, that was the submarine. Seconds passed and he heard and felt the heavy double shock of their explosion.

"Yippee!" shrilled the voice of the tail gunner. "You sure smacked him, Windy!"

Owens brought the ship around in a tight turn and they saw the churned-up patch of ocean where the bombs had struck. Suddenly, right in the middle of it, a dark steel object broke water—the battered conning tower of a submarine.

"Surfacing!" cried half a dozen of the crew. "You've got him in trouble, boy! Must have damaged his controls!"

"What do you say, Windy? Want to bomb again?" That was the pilot's voice.

"Let's see what he aims to do. Don't want to waste eggs."

"That's right," called the tail gunner. "Give us boys a

chance!"

The Liberator circled again and came in low over the disabled submarine. Tiny figures were swarming out on her narrow deck. The forward gun was out of commission, twisted over at a crazy angle on its base. As the plane passed overhead some of the sailors were trying to elevate the machine gun aft of the conning tower, but a sharp burst from the twin fifty-calibers in the bomber's tail dropped two of them and the others ran for shelter.

Barney was staring, eyes wide, mouth open. On the torn and riddled side of the U-boat's superstructure he saw the painted coils of a cobra, and a number that he would never forget. "Gosh!" he gasped. "It's the *Sea Snake*—the U-432! It's the sub I was on!"

The plane swooped low over the deck once more, and they could see men trying to inflate a rubber life-raft. A little figure in the uniform of an officer was wildly waving a white cloth that looked like a bed sheet.

"Hold your fire, gunners," ordered Owens. "He's trying to surrender!"

The Liberator continued to circle watchfully. At the end of two or three minutes the submarine was so down by the stern that her shark-like bow thrust upward helplessly above the waves. All of the crew but one man and the smartly attired officer had packed themselves into the rubber boat. The bomber was so close that Barney could see their white, strained faces, upturned in fear. Then he recognized the two figures still clinging to the tilted deck. They were Lieutenant Rasch and Blohm, the bosun. Blohm seemed to be pleading with his commander, urging him toward the boat, and Rasch was hesitating. At that instant there was a muffled explosion somewhere deep in the submarine's hull. The bow heaved suddenly upward, the conning tower disappeared, and both men were hurled into the swirling maelstrom of sea that surrounded the foundering craft.

For a second or two the black bow hung poised above them, then vanished beneath the surface, sucking their bobbing heads after it. There was nothing the crew of the plane could do but watch the grim drama below and clench their teeth.

The life raft was nearly swamped by the rush of water, but somehow it kept right side up. The men who had gone under never reappeared.

"Get that radio hot," the pilot's voice grated. "Find those destroyers an' tell 'em we've got fifty Heinie prisoners we don't know what to do with. If they're really pourin' oil like

U432

they said, they ought to be pretty close."

Nate began sending at once. As the answer came back he relayed it to Owens. "They're only twenty miles northeast. Say they'll pick these boys up in half an hour. Seem a little surprised about our takin' prisoners, though."

The Captain chuckled. "Well, folks," he said, "looks like we've got to play nurse-maid here for a spell. Anybody know any parlor games?"

They circled monotonously above the bobbing raft, never letting it get more than a mile or two away. Barney borrowed Windy's binoculars and studied the huddled Germans whenever they were close enough. He picked out several men he knew—young Hans and Froelich among others. There was nobody in the group bulky enough to be the cook. Perhaps the fat man had been unable to hoist himself up the ladder in the rush after the U-boat was hit.

"They didn't all get off," the boy announced. "All I can count is thirty-five or thirty-six. That's a dozen short— maybe more. An' some of 'em are in bad shape. One man's got a broken leg, looks like. She must have got hit at Atlantic City an' tried to make it back here. That's why she was surfaced in daylight."

Soon they saw a double smoke cloud on the horizon, and

the lean gray ships came racing into view.

"Sort o' pretty, aren't they?" said Windy grudgingly. "But who wants to crawl around on the ocean at forty miles an hour?"

The leading destroyer signaled rapidly with its blinker and Nate read the code. "Commander says he plans to do his attacking at the island right away. Wants to know if we're taking part."

"Tell him we'll act under his orders, but we've only got gas for about five more hours. He'll need to know how to get through the reef, though. Tell him the opening's just east of north—around five degrees. Here, you'd better take Barney's sketch-map and read off the points of interest, like the U-boat berth by the dock and that white stone building back under the trees."

The wireless buzzed steadily while the prisoners were being taken aboard the destroyer.

"All right," said Nate at last. "Here's all the dope. He figures they've got that passage through the reef mined, so he'll shell from outside. Wants us to run over and drop a bomb or two as near their headquarters as we can. He's set the time for fourteen forty-five."

The destroyers roared off southeastward and the Liberator

loafed above them, swinging in wide, lazy circles to keep the ships in sight.

"Well, boys," said Owens, casually. "Maybe in another hour or so you'll know what ack-ack fire is like."

# 19

THE destroyers went in first. Five miles astern and 15,000 feet above the sea, the big B-24 circled, waiting for the battle to begin. Through the binoculars, Barney could see the fighting ships like steel lance-heads on the long white shafts of their wakes.

They were close to the reef and slackening their speed now. One had swung west, skirting the line of surf. The other was at the entrance to the lagoon. A slow white puff of smoke blossomed from the forward guns of the nearer destroyer and the palm trees by the long pier went into a sudden convulsion. Even before the thud of the report reached the plane the other ship opened fire on the thick cover where the headquarters buildings were hidden.

The salvos came in quick succession from the smartly handled guns. It was four or five minutes before there was

any return fire, and then it came from a single gun, camou-
flaged at the edge of the lagoon. Barney saw the smoke, and
then the white water-spout of a shell that passed over the
farther ship's deck. Almost instantly the destroyer's battery
was trained on the shore gun. Splinters and debris flew into
the air and the Germans did not fire again.

"Reckon it's about time we did our job," said Captain
Owens. "She's all yours, Windy."

The bombardier braced his shoulders. "Here we go," he
answered. "Come down a couple o' thousand an' take her
straight in."

Once again he set his dials, watching the approaching target through his bombsight. "You're dead on it," he called.
"Dead on it—as she goes!"

The bomb doors slapped open and a few seconds later he
pressed the release. "Bombs away!"

Before Barney could draw breath there was a crash and
the plane jolted violently. Around them he saw a dozen
bursting puffs of gray smoke. The Liberator hurtled upward
into a wing-over turn and began a series of diving zigzags.
For a moment the boy clung white-faced to his seat. He
thought they had been hit and were falling, out of control.
Then he realized dizzily that the ack-ack puffs were farther

off. The giant plane was ducking and dodging to avoid the ground gunners' aim. Two minutes later she was clear out of range.

"Phew!" Windy sighed and wiped his brow, grinning at Barney. "So that's what it's like! Some ride you gave us, Jack. Any damage?"

"Nothing serious that I can see. How 'bout you boys? Check in."

One by one they answered. All the crew were present and accounted for. The gunner in the top blister reported a few holes in the left wing and a slug through the fuselage, but no damage to any vital part. "There's gas comin' out o' that wing tank, though," he added.

Owens turned over the controls to Slug and went aft to look. When he came back a moment later his voice was sober. "Sorry, boys," he said. "We can't stay to see the fun. Got to head for home. If your radio's working, Nate, you'd better tell the Commander and find out how they're doing back there. By the way, did anybody see those bombs hit?"

"Yeah!" It was the tail gunner talking. "Just about the time you went into that bank. Got one buildin' anyhow, for there was some stone an' timbers flyin'."

The radioman buzzed away for several minutes, with intermittent pauses for replies from the Commander's destroyer, now many miles behind them and over the rim of the sea.

When he finally shut off the transmitter they heard him draw a deep breath. "Seems to be about over, Jack," he reported. "No more gunfire ashore an' the Jerries act like they're getting ready to surrender. He says our bombs were a big help. An' the gobs put a shell in that ammunition dump. Nearly blew up the whole island."

"Good enough!" said the pilot. "Now everybody check your parachutes, because there's about an even chance you'll have to bail out before we can land. The gas is all gone out o' that shot-up wing and even with the mixture leaned down we're running pretty short. You can tell Miami that, Nate. Keep sending our position and ask 'em to have a boat ready if we ask for it. I may decide to put her down on the water instead."

Nobody had much to say during that next hour. Windy tried once or twice to make cheerful conversation but his efforts fell flat. Barney wasn't exactly scared. He just wondered what it was like to bail out of a plane with a parachute.

"I never used one o' these things," he remarked into the microphone. "Isn't there a ring you're supposed to pull?"

The bombardier nodded understandingly. "That one right there," he pointed. "But the main thing is to fall clear before you pull it. Count ten after you jump. Then there's nothing to it except the jerk when she opens. I'll go first anyhow, so you'll see how it's done."

But Barney wasn't fated to join the caterpillar club that day. Just about the time the fuel gauge registered empty they sighted the Florida coast, and with one motor dead and the others sputtering, Jack Owens brought the *Chattanooga Choo-Choo* in to a perfect landing.

*　　*　　*

It was early the next afternoon when Barney and Slug Martin got off the transport plane at Washington. A big black car with U. S. Navy tags was waiting for them, and the officer who ushered them into it was a grizzled Captain with three bars of service ribbons and a Navy cross on his breast.

"We got the orders to repo't, suh," said Slug diffidently, "but I'd be right interested to know where you're takin' us."

The four-striper smiled. "I believe it won't be a very unpleasant ordeal," he answered. "The Secretary wants to meet this young man, and since you've been detailed to look after him, you're likewise invited. Quite a successful little affair you took part in yesterday. There'll be nothing in the papers of course, but all the men left on the base were taken prisoners, in case you hadn't heard."

The car whirled along the broad streets of the capital and the driver brought it to a gliding stop by a gate in a wrought-iron fence.

"Here we are," said the naval officer briskly.

Barney saw a wide sweep of lawn and a stately building with pillared porticoes. Beside him Slug gave a little gasp. "I've never been here," he whispered. "But this isn't the Navy Department. It's—it's the—"

"We'll go in this side entrance," the Captain announced. He nodded to the guards. "These are the special visitors," he said. "I'm responsible for them."

He led the way along a handsome corridor and knocked at a high, paneled door. It was opened by a middle-aged man with a tired face who brightened visibly when he saw who the guests were. "Hello, Joe," he said. "They're just through lunch and ready for you. Come right along in."

A pair of solid-looking men in civilian clothes were standing in the first room they entered. Barney felt uncomfortable under their sharp scrutiny but he followed along at the heels of his guide. The inner room was big and bright with sun-light. There was a huge desk, covered with statuettes, ship models and other knickknacks. A Scotty dog rose deliberately and inspected the newcomers.

Suddenly Barney's step faltered as he looked at the two men seated behind the desk. One was a sturdy, ruddy-faced gentleman, wearing eye-glasses. And the other—he would have recognized him anywhere—was the President of the United States!

"Mr. President—Mr. Secretary," their sponsor smiled, "I'd like to present Mr. Cannon and Lieutenant Martin. You already know the Captain."

In a daze Barney moved forward to shake first one, then the other, of the outstretched hands.

"Pull up chairs for them, Steve," said the President. "We're not going to be rushed about this. Nobody likes a good sea yarn better than I do, and I believe this boy's got one to tell."

In a moment Barney felt wholly at his ease. Under their friendly questioning he forgot his awe and began to talk. During the next half hour he told them the whole story of his adventure. Several times the President nodded delightedly.

"Great!" he exclaimed when the boy finished. "Wiping out that base will save us a lot of ships—a lot of seamen's lives, and cargoes we can't spare. But about that chemical—what did you find on that, Captain?"

The naval officer looked thoughtful. "It's hard to say, sir, just yet. We've got the analysis, and we're going to try making it in experimental quantities. So far we can't be sure, but it looks as if we'd eventually be able to get pure hydrogen and oxygen from water, when we've discovered the right proportions to use."

The Secretary of the Navy thumped the arm of his chair with his fist. "No wonder they've fooled us—able to cruise for months that way, while we've been scouring the Atlantic for their tankers!"

Barney saw the President's eyes twinkle. "Seems to me you owe this lad something, Frank," he said. "He looks about the right age to get into the Navy. How old are you, son?"

Barney reddened. "I'll be seventeen right soon. Reckon my birthday's next week. But—well, you see, sir—I've sort o' hoped I could be an Army flier like Sl— like Lieutenant Martin, here."

The President rocked back in his chair and roared with

laughter. "Serves us right, Frank!" he said. "The boy has his own plans. And I, for one, say he's entitled to them."

He turned to Barney again. "You find out where the nearest Aviation Cadet Examining Board is," he told him. "When you're seventeen you can take your examinations and get into the Air Force Enlisted Reserve. You have to have your parents' consent, of course, but I expect they'll be delighted."

"Yes, sir," Barney nodded. "That's what I was figuring to do. Only first I've got to finish out my high school and do a heap o' studying so I can pass those examinations."

"More power to you!" said the Commander-in-Chief, shaking hands with him again. "I'm going to see you get some recognition for this job you've done, even if it takes an act of Congress. Write to me once in a while and tell me how you're getting on."

*　　*　　*

Outside, moving toward the White House gate, Barney still felt as if his feet were treading on air.

"Well," said the Captain, "that wasn't so bad, was it? Tell me, gentlemen. Is there any place you'd like to be taken?"

"We-all are mighty indebted to you, suh," said Slug, "but I reckon Barney's in sort of a swivet to get home an' see his folks. So maybe the railroad station—"

"We'll do better than that," the Captain grinned. "There's a new Billy Mitchell bomber out at the Field, waiting to be flown down to Kitty Hawk. I believe you've had some experience in twin-engine ships?"

"Yes, suh!" Slug beamed. "Lead me to her!"

In half an hour they were streaking southeastward with the whole of Chesapeake Bay and Tidewater Virginia unrolling beneath them.

The runways at the coastal base had been lengthened since Barney saw them last, and Slug brought the fast bomber down in a perfect landing. The Commanding Officer gave them both a hearty greeting. "By the way, Martin," he said, "your leave isn't up till midnight, if there's anything you'd like to do."

"Yes, suh. Thank you, suh," the pilot grinned. He commandeered a jeep and he and Barney trundled off down the road.

The dunes were golden in the late afternoon sun and a breeze came gently from the south. The boy could hear the low roar of the surf, the cry of the gulls. He had a lump in his throat when at last the tough little car slithered through the sand and stopped at the familiar doorway.

There was a tramp of heavy boots coming up from the dock. John Cannon stood there, big and burly in his weather-beaten dungarees. Slowly he wiped the fish-scales off his hand on his thigh and came forward.

"Well—I'll be dawg!" was all he said, but there was moisture in the wrinkles at the corners of his blue eyes. He gripped Barney's hand in his own calloused paw and held it tight as he led him toward the house.

The door flew open then. Mrs. Cannon had caught sight of her son and she came out with skirt and apron billowing like the sails of a schooner before the wind.

"Barney!" she gasped. "My goodness—you look pale as a ghost! I don't s'pose you've sat down to a square meal since you left here. Anna! Put another place at the table—two more places. Good thing I made plenty o' that chowder, an' supper's most ready now."

She gave the boy a great hug and rushed back to the cook-stove.

"Pete's done enlisted in the Coast Guard," said his father. "But here's somebody else might be glad to see you."

Barney caught a glimpse of a flushed, excited face inside the door, and the next instant Anna flung her arms about his neck. "*Ach!*" she sobbed. "You did come back, Barney. I thought—never—those Nazis—"

"Here—g-gosh!" he stammered. "Quit that, Anna! I wouldn't have missed all that's happened for anything. An' guess who I shook hands with today. The President! Honest Injun!"

The table was quickly set and the big bowls of chowder came steaming from the kettle. They took their places and bowed their heads. John Cannon's sea-going voice rumbled a sober grace.

"Dear Lord an' Father, we-all thank Thee for this yeah food we're aimin' to eat. An' we thank Thee for takin' good care of our boy through all the perils he's done been in, on land an' under the sea. An' bless us an' keep us all, them as ain't with us tonight an' them as is. We ask it in Jesus' name. Amen."

He paused briefly. "Well, son," he went on in matter-of-fact tones as he tucked his napkin under his chin, "fish been bitin' good an' it looks like a fair day tomorrow. Reckon you'll be goin' out with me in the ol' *Jennie May?*"

"Reckon I will," said Barney happily.

**THE END**